THE UNTIMELY DEATH OF IVY TUCKER

Book 3 of the Kate Nash Series

SUSAN KEENE

Publishing Coordinator – Sharon Kizziah-Holmes

Published by Bent Willow Books

ISBN -13: 978-1-945669-94-1

ACKNOWLEDGMENTS

I would like to thank the Pen Gypsies, Sharon Kizziah-Holmes, Tierney James, and Shirley McCann. These fantastic friends and writers are always there to help work out a plot problem.

Thanks to the FBI, US Marshall Service, local law enforcement and of course, my family.

Small acts when multiplied by millions of people,
can transform the world.

CHAPTER 1

Kate, tell me one more time what happened."
I became more frustrated by the moment. I cried before the police arrived and held back tears since. "Roger, what more can I say? I came downstairs, opened the door to step out and pick up the Sunday paper. As I opened the door, the body fell inside."

Roger Simon, lead detective from the St. Louis Homicide Division knelt next to the body on our stoop for the third time. "She looks so young and little. There isn't a mark on her body."

Ryan, my boyfriend of many years, stood quietly off to the side of the porch. "Call your CSI team so we can go inside. We're drawing a crowd." Roger looked up and around as if he hadn't noticed. Ryan put his hands on his hips. "You can't barrel down the street in a quiet neighborhood that has virtually no crime, sirens blasting, and not draw any attention to yourself."

I was Roger's old partner and friend of fifteen years. His inability to accept the dead body half on the porch and half in our foyer agitated me more and more as he went over it again and again. I no longer tried to hide my irritation. "Roger, I know it is your job to be thorough, but as I told you before, we didn't hear, see, or smell anything. My guess is, someone put her here early this morning before the neighbors were up and about. I think whoever killed the girl wanted her found. Why else dump her on someone's front porch? We both know there are a million empty fields and isolated areas where they could have put her."

The detective unfolded to his full height of six-feet-six and stretched. "Okay, I'll call— Kate, you can go inside. I'll be in as soon as the crew gets here and we square this away." I started to walk toward the door but turned back to talk to him. "If you're coming in to visit or have coffee, you're more than welcome. If you're intending to ask more redundant questions, you can mosey on. Our day has already gone in a different direction than we had planned. But do let us know who she is and how she died."

I knew I sounded cold and unfeeling. It was far from the truth. The girl couldn't have been over twenty-five. Her long auburn hair lay around her face. She looked radiant even in death, but I spent enough time in the limelight to last me a lifetime and people had begun to gather.

Roger looked from me to Ryan and back. "That's a bit curt don't you think? Come on guys. I'm not accusing you of anything. Don't you think it's strange a young woman happened to pick your front steps to die on?"

Before we could answer, an ambulance, a crime scene van, and three more patrol cars rolled up, sirens blasting, and lights twirling red and blue. Roger talked to them. "Bag her hands and feet. Take her in. Block this yard off as a crime scene. Make sure you rope off the entire front. I don't want anybody stepping on clues.

I reached up and tapped him on the shoulder. "Roger. We've only lived here a couple of months. I'm sure you remember the big scene when we were arrested in front of this very house before we moved in. The neighbors would be within their rights to go before the Association and ask us to move. We love this place."

Ryan, who stood with his arms crossed, spoke up. "Come on. We're all adults here. We're not expecting company, and we don't know the people on the block. No one will contaminate your crime scene. By the time you leave your men will have combed this place three times. Can't you just take the body and go? We'll be here all day, alone. Call us later."

Roger turned his attention to the two men who put the body on the stretcher. "This was under the body, Captain." One of them handed him a piece of folded paper.

He put on a pair of surgical gloves before he opened it. "It says, *Kate Nash, Private Investigator* and your address here and at the Clayton office. Folded with it are a couple of articles. One about how you found Lizzy Smith and the other about discovering you had a twin sister. Looks like you had a fan."

Ryan and I stood close to him so we could see the items for ourselves. "I haven't got a clue," I said, "there is always the chance she died of natural causes, although I doubt it."

"Me either." Ryan echoed.

Roger refolded the note and newspaper stories and put it inside an evidence bag. "I guess I'll come in for that cup of coffee." He turned around to the team. "Tape off this yard, the entire front of the house from the driveway to the sidewalk out front." He glanced back toward Ryan and me but didn't look us in the eye.

I knew he had a job to do and he would do it to the best of his ability, by the rules. The tape off the crime scene rule was a biggy.

Ten minutes later the doorbell rang. Ryan went to answer it. He came back followed by my business partner and best friend, Amy Perkin and her boyfriend Nathan, who was Ryan's second in command. Digger, Amy's dog, lounged in her arms.

Chili, my mini dachshund, who had been asleep on my lap, jumped down to greet her buddy.

We were at the dining room table. Amy pulled out a chair and sat next to Roger. Nathan sat on the other side of Ryan.

So much for salvaging any part of the day to spend alone with Ryan. I tried to sound cheerful. "I didn't expect to see you two until tomorrow. Is anything wrong?"

Amy poured herself a cup of coffee from the

carafe on the table and gestured toward Nathan to see if he wanted one. "We heard the news and thought we should come over to make sure you're okay."

"What news?" I asked.

Nathan reached for a cup. "The dead girl on the porch, it's all over the radio and TV. You're famous. You know you can't go anywhere without the paparazzi on your tail. You definitely can't find a body on your stoop and not have it all over the news."

Ryan, Roger, and I all said, *great*, in unison.

Roger shook his head. "So much for my crime scene not being contaminated. Did you guys jump the tape?"

No one answered him.

Amy reached down and picked up Chili who jumped at her legs to get attention. "What do you know about the dead girl?"

"She's young, dead, and there's not a mark on her visible to the naked eye. She had a note, it said *if anyone could help her, I could,* and it had this address and the office address. She also had some stories cut from the newspaper about two of our past cases. Her name was Marie. You answer the phone more than I do. Did anyone named Marie call the office?"

Amy reached down again to pick up Digger. Now she had two puppies in her arms but didn't seem to mind. "No one by the name Marie called."

I had a twinge of sadness, to die so young, and alone.

Roger's phone rang; he left the table to answer it.

When he came back, he asked for a glass of water. "She had a driver's license in her pocket issued to a Marie Ann Ripley. There's no record of a Marie Ann Ripley anywhere near her age, no social security number, no record of birth— nothing. There's no such address as the one listed on her ID. It is an empty lot on the bad side of Granite City. The men are checking with the Illinois authorities to see if they have a missing person who fits her description."

"They'll do a tox-screen to see if she was drugged—or drugged herself. The Medical Examiner said she was in her twenties and had never had children. I guess we're at a standstill for now, unless something comes back from the lab tests or the autopsy. We'll run her DNA, but we all know how long that takes. I'll leave you folks to enjoy the rest of your day. I'll grab the crime scene tape on my way out. However, I insist we have an unmarked car in front of the house since we don't have a clue what all this is about."

"Roger, save the taxpayers' money. One of my guys will do the surveillance. I'll have someone here twenty-four-seven," Ryan said.

"Thanks, let me know if anything comes from the stakeout."

Ryan stood to walk him to the door. "You'll be the first to know."

Nathan made the call and had a car on the way before Ryan got back to the kitchen. "Let's go outside. The patio's in the shade and the dogs can run around. I know you ladies well enough to know you don't intend to let this go. I'm sure you'll know her real name before Roger does."

Amy unfolded her long lanky legs from under the chair and put both dogs on the floor before she stood. "You do protection. We solve crimes. Just like it was in your nature to use your own men to watch us and the house, it's our nature to try to figure out who she was, and what she wanted with our agency." She glanced down over her lime green granny glasses and added, "and who killed her."

Beautiful described Amy to a tee. She didn't need make up. Her tight and smooth skin had the same tone, winter and summer. The blush on her cheeks accented her high cheekbones. All of her clothes were bright colors and fit her like a glove. Around her neck she wore a pair of cheaters on a cord. The glasses and chain of the day always matched some item of her clothing. Today they matched perfectly with the designs on her blouse. I know she had a pair in every color.

I went to the wine chiller and grabbed a bottle of Chardonnay and four glasses. When I came back I asked, "So you have already made up your mind its a murder?"

Nathan took the glasses out of my hand. "She looked awfully healthy for it to be anything else. Did you get a glimpse of her arm and leg muscles? Looks like she ran and lifted weights. I guess there's nothing for us to do right now but wait."

Ryan went inside to see what kind of snacks we had. "How did you see her? I thought she had been taken away by the time you got here."

Nathan filled the wine glasses all around. "The ambulance drivers were standing by the door. She hadn't been put in the back yet. We walked up like we belonged and pulled the sheet down to take a look at her."

"Okay," I said, "since the day didn't go as planned, let's make the most of it. How about lunch on the grill and we enjoy this beautiful day. It's after one, I'm hungry."

Ryan came by and kissed me on the top of the head. He laid an unopened potato chip bag on the table. "I knew I loved you for a reason. It's that sharp mind of yours. Are ribeyes okay with everyone? Want me to whip up a salad?"

Ryan was a good cook and he liked the chore. He and I had been friends since college, dated for a few years, moved in together, and had been happy so far. He wanted to get married. I had been wearing his mother's ring for almost a year. I couldn't muster up the courage to take the final step. One day I would, I knew it.

During the entire meal, I couldn't get my mind off Marie. Who was she? I wished Roger would call with some new information.

Like magic, my cell phone rang. "Nash here." People asked why I answered my phone the same way every time. My standard answer was, '*cause I'm Nash and I'm here.*

"We ran the girl's fingerprints through Codis. She showed up as a missing person in 2008, Ivy Rose Tucker. She was eleven the last time she was seen alive. She and her family were from Chicago. Her parents were doctors. Her mother, Sharon, a neurosurgeon age 37, and her father, Eric, a pediatrician age 39. She had a younger sister,

Dallas, age 9 and an older brother, Maxwell, age 17. They went on an extended cruise to the Gulf of California and to explore the Mexican mainland. They arrive at their first destination. No one reported seeing or hearing from them again. Still no cause of death on Ivy."

"Thanks. You don't care if we dig into this, do you? After all, she had our agency card with her."

He laughed, not a funny laugh but a resigned one. "Is there any way I could stop you? As usual, all of my resources are at your disposal. Tell Ryan not to hack any government computers this time. If I find out anything else, I'll let you know."

I passed the information on to the group. A chill ran up my spine. I wish I knew the cause of death. It made a big difference to me since she was found at our house.

Ryan leaned over and put his hand on mine. "I don't know if my feelings should be hurt because you would rather investigate this murder than spend the next week as we planned. I have known you two long enough," he smiled at Amy, "not to take it personally. Nathan and I will do all we can to help solve this. It seems to me we should wait until we have a cause of death before we form a plan of action. Right now, for all we know, she could have had a heart attack."

CHAPTER 2

O ur curiosity, and what it would take to launch a full-blown investigation into the girl's death, came nowhere close to each other. The four of us were intrigued but unwilling to start a new case on a beautiful, lazy Sunday afternoon. I had been busy with a case that involved my mother and sister. I had gone to bed every night since then with the realization my entire life had been a lie. It monopolized my thoughts. A new case might help me crawl out of the dark.

For the second time in the same day, I felt as if someone had a listening device in my mind. Amy asked about my sister, Sarah. "Is your sister thriving as the new boss of the De Marco Crime Family?"

I gave her my biggest smile. "They have it almost turned around, of course no matter how much good they do, someone will find out it used to be the De Marco *family business*. Tony has been in culinary school and is working at the Seafood Palace. Our *so-called* mother and Uncle Dominic are safely tucked away in a Federal Prison. I doubt they ever see the outside world again.

"I'd say Tony and Sarah are living the dream. Think of the good you could do with a hundred million dollars."

Amy laughed. "I think of the good I could do with an extra thousand. I doubt either of us will ever get to find out."

Nathan stood to refill Ryan's wine glass. "The only other good thing to come out of that case was Ryan putting you into the background check business. You could never do another outside case and have more money than before."

Amy and I looked at one another. "I find it boring," Amy said.

I raised my glass to get attention and more wine. "Me too, but for the first time, we can work on the Ivy Tucker case and not worry about whether we have the money to pay the bills."

Roger called one more time. "There were two other people on the Tucker boat, a Captain, Michael Mannes and his wife, Janis, who served as a cook and all-around helper. She was thirty-six, he was thirty-nine, neither of them was ever seen or heard from again."

"Since Ivy showed up after ten years, it makes me wonder if all of the rest of them are actually dead." I looked around the room for approval of what I was about to say. "I think we had best begin in Chicago and see who these people were. Things might not be as they seem."

Before he hung up, Roger added, "...in murder cases they seldom are."

Amy had both dogs next to her. "Let's get back to background checks. I counted Friday. We have a hundred and forty in the office as we speak. EDP has sixty waiting. They want everything including which side of the bed the prospective employee sleeps on. They take almost a day a piece. Marky Mart hardly wants anything. I think they'll hire anyone who's breathing. We have to get them done. We're getting spoiled with this steady income."

Ryan sat next to me on the swing. "Tell you what. I know you wouldn't let me help with the money end before, but now that you wear my ring, I hope you will. My guys like to stay busy. Since we are nationwide, I sometimes have more men than work. Nathan can set your computers so the names of those being checked go straight to Jacob at the tech desk. He'll pass them out and get them done. You can spend as much time on Ivy Tucker as you wish."

I looked over to Amy who had a big grin on her face. "I would love that. Of course, we will give you a percentage of the money for doing the work."

Ryan shook his head. "Did you get the part where I don't think we have to go tit for tat on the money thing anymore? Why bother? Everything I have is half Kate's now."

"It is?"

"Yes, I love you more than anyone and I don't know who else I would leave it to. If I leave large sums to charity the CEOs just get richer."

Ryan was one of the three richest men in

Missouri. One man ran a brewery, another family owned an auto rental company. Ryan owned the largest home security business in the country. Lately, he had branched out to commercial companies. He owned several restaurants, an art gallery, and a minor league basketball team, oh yes, and forty acres and a mansion a stone's throw from Forest Park. He had turned the acreage into a public garden and the house into a museum.

If you met him on the street, he would be the last man you thought had that kind of money.

His mother and father were killed in an automobile accident when he was sixteen. I and several other friends became his family. He had mothered us for the past fifteen years. At last count, he was the Godfather to seventeen children.

I put my hand on his leg and turned to kiss his cheek. "I'm good with that. When I think of all of the cases I've read about and not been able to investigate because we needed to find a lost cat or a wandering husband so we could keep the bills paid."

Nathan and Amy left about nine. It wasn't the way I intended to spend my day, but except for the dead body on the porch, I enjoyed it.

Ryan walked toward the sliding door. "Let's sit on the deck. I don't know how many cool nights are in our future. Summer is coming on fast."

Chili heard the door open and headed outside on a dead run. I laughed and followed her. "Should we be nervous a body showed up on the porch. I wonder what the chances are she was killed where she laid? And I can't imagine where she's been for the last ten years? Wonder why she changed her name?"

We didn't have a chance to discuss it. Ryan's phone rang. He hung up then told me, "Get the dog, we need to meet Nathan at the hospital. Someone attacked him and Amy as they walked up to her door."

"Are they okay?"

"I think so. Nathan is upset he couldn't protect his girlfriend. Amy is asking for you."

The trip to the hospital was quiet. I didn't have anything to say until I found out what happened. There were worry lines on Ryan's face.

Nathan met us at the emergency room door. He had a deep cut over his right eye, and a bump the size of a golf ball on the back of his head. He didn't give us a chance to ask a question. "I walked Amy to the door and when I turned around to leave, I heard her scream. She fell to the ground. I couldn't see anyone yet someone hit me on the back of the head. I cut my eye when I fell."

Ryan put his hand on his friend's shoulder. "Let's sit down. How's Amy?"

Nathan ran both hands through his curly brown hair. "I'm not sure. She was injected with something. The emergency room doctor found a small hole behind her ear. They don't know what it was. She's throwing up and in and out of consciousness. When she wakes up she smiles at me but asks to see you, Kate."

"I had better get in there," I said.

Two doctors and a nurse stood over her. The nurse looked at me. "You must be Kate. Your friend is very sick. We have determined she was injected with a toxin of some sort. According to a preliminary blood test, we believe it was a venom."

I walked closer to Amy, but her eyes were closed. "How will you know what to give her if you don't know what it was?"

One of the men who had been talking with another in the corner, walked over to where I stood. "I'm Dr. Sanchez. I believe your friend was injected with the venom of a Coral Snake. The emergency room doctor called me in because I was raised on the Baja Peninsula and have seen this poisoning many times. There is no anti-venom for this type of snake bite. The companies stopped making it. In this case, I don't think your friend received enough to kill her.

"We have given her massive doses of antihistamines which explains why she is asleep. Don't get alarmed, but we are moving her to ICU and will put her on a ventilator, at least for tonight, maybe even tomorrow. We will see. One of the main causes of death from this snake is the person's inability to breathe without help. Hopefully, we can stop that symptom before it begins.

"She is to go to the other unit within the next ten minutes. Give us an hour to get her situated and comfortable and you can each see her one more time tonight. After that, I suggest you go home. Your friend is not going to wake up. If there is any change, we will call you." He ushered me out of the room.

Ryan stood in the doorway of one of the ER treatment rooms. I walked over and stood next to him. "Hi, how's Amy?"

"They think she was injected with the venom of a Coral Snake. They are moving her to ICU."

He hugged me. "Honey, I'm so sorry. I'll get on the phone, find a specialist and fly him here."

"I'm afraid. I don't believe we need a specialist. One of her doctors is from the Baja and is familiar with the poison. He has it all under control."

Ryan walked off, phone in hand. I took his place and watched over Nathan while they put five stitches above his eye.

He noticed me. "What did you learn?"

"The poison was from a Coral Snake. The doctor doesn't think it was enough to kill her. They are moving her to ICU."

I had never seen Nathan with the expression of despair on his face I saw when I gave him the news. "Can I see her?"

I repeated what Dr. Sanchez shared with me. We waited silently for Ryan.

CHAPTER 3

While we waited to see Amy in the ICU, I called Roger. "I thought I would let you know Amy and Nathan were mugged when he took her home tonight."

"Do you have any idea who or why?"

What a dumb question, I thought, although I didn't say as much. "Let's see, a body on the porch and an attack a few hours later. I'd say they were connected, but I know how to find out for sure. Amy was injected with Coral Snake venom. Ask your medical examiner to check for the same thing in Ivy Tucker's blood."

" Coral Snake venom is a little out of the ordinary isn't it? When did this happen?"

"I think about ten. They left our house after nine."

"How are they?"

I began to tear up. "Nathan is okay except for a

knot on the back of the head and a cut over his eye. Amy is in intensive care on a respirator in case the medicine they gave her doesn't work. They said they would put her on a breathing machine to override the effects of the poison. We were told there is no anti-venom for the coral snake. I pray they are on the right path."

I heard Roger take a deep breath. "I'll send a crew and a couple of officers to her house. Give me a few minutes to get dressed and make the calls and I'll be there. Where are you?"

"St. Mary's."

He hung up without another word. I went back to where the men waited to see if there was any change in Amy's condition. It had been over two hours and no one had come to talk to us again nor did we get to see her. All we did was wait and take turns pacing and looking through the small window in the door. They had the curtain drawn over the big window on our side. It was gut-wrenching. We all tried not to let our imaginations run wild, but it was a difficult task.

Fifteen minutes later Dr. Sanchez came from the nurse's station and talked to us. I introduced him to Ryan and Nathan. "Your friend is much better. The venom she received is unpredictable though. It can play havoc with the respiratory system. I think the safest thing to do is keep her on the ventilator. You can go in for a few minutes but then it would be best if you go home. There is nothing you can do here and she will remain sedated through tomorrow so she doesn't pull out the breathing tube."

Ryan stood between Nathan and me. He pulled

Nathan closer to him and squeezed his shoulder. "We understand. We'll leave our phone numbers. If anything changes. Please call."

The doctor stood aside and let the three of us into the room. It was cold and dark. Ryan and I stayed back to let Nathan move closer to Amy. "Can you hear me. I'm here. You're going to be fine. Ryan and Kate are here. They won't let us stay but if you need us, we'll be right back. I love you, Amy."

I stepped up and kissed her on the cheek, Ryan stood rooted in the same spot.

A nurse came in and told us we had to leave. Nathan kissed her lightly and we walked out into the hall.

Before we got to the waiting room Roger came in. "Amy's house is covered. We found this." He held up a small evidence bag with what looked to be a dart in it.

Ryan reached for the bag. "Is this how he got the venom in her?"

Roger took it from him and handed it to Nathan. "We think so. I think he loaded it full of poison and tried to stab her with it. When she screamed, he threw it down or dropped it. His only objective then was to get out of there. He was in such a hurry he walked out of one of his shoes. It's with the crime team. I'm hoping there is DNA on the dart. I don't believe I have ever seen a blow dart up close."

I shook my head. "This doesn't make sense. Why come after us? Never mind. I know why. Whoever he, or they are, they don't know how long we knew Ivy. He doesn't know if we'd met Ivy before and she told us a story or if when he killed her we hadn't had a chance to talk to her yet. There's something he doesn't want anyone to know. He can't take the chance that we already know whatever his secret is so he came after us.

"Why Nathan and Amy, why not Ryan and me? I hate it Amy is suffering due to something she isn't even involved in."

Ryan pulled out his phone. We could hear his conversation. "Dennis, sorry to wake you but we have a job. I'll need your entire group. Please move quickly on this. I need two men at St. Mary's Hospital on Clayton Road. I want you to sit outside room two in the intensive care unit. No matter what, don't leave the door unattended.

"I want three of you to go to 1311 Mathews Court in the city. I want one of you to do a drive by every fifteen minutes. Change drivers and cars every three trips. One of you watch the front of the house and one watch the back.

Lastly, send three men to my house. Al is already there, let him go home. Put them where you think they will do the most good. I do want someone to make the circle around the block every fifteen minutes. If anyone sees anything, no matter how small, I want to hear about it."

Roger tapped him on the shoulder and he added, "… and call 911. Tell them to notify homicide."

Roger slipped the evidence bag in his pocket and took out a small notepad. "Nathan, can you tell me anything about the man who assaulted you?"

"No. I actually thought Amy was inside. I never leave before she's inside and closes the door. Something must have brought her back out. If he tapped on the door, she would have thought it was me and opened it without hesitation."

Roger looked him in the eye. "Do you often go back after you have said goodnight?"

Nathan's face turned crimson. He looked at me, then Ryan, and back to the man questioning him. "Only when one of us changes our mind about me spending the night.

"It happened quickly. Amy was on the ground holding a hand over the back of her neck and moaning. When I knelt to see what happened, someone clobbered me. I don't know what he used but it was heavy. Because of how low the wound on the back of my head is, I think he is shorter than me. I got this gash over my eye I when I fell. I must have hit one of the decorative bricks she has around the flower bed."

Roger tapped his pen on the pad he held. "So what are you, about six-feet-three? The perp could have been six feet and not been able to reach the top of your head if the item he struck you with was heavy enough. You said you knelt to see if Amy was okay. So, when he hit you, were you standing or kneeling?"

Nathan shook his head. "I must have still been on my knees. Sorry. My mind is on Amy."

"Not a problem. We found a garden gnome with blood on it. We'll run it and see if it's your blood and maybe get lucky with one of his fingerprints."

Ryan stood with his arms crossed over his chest and moved his head back and forth as if he were watching a tennis match as Nathan and Roger talked. "You said you found a shoe. What kind?"

"The label reads Manuel Sekkel. Are you familiar with the brand?"

Ryan stepped forward. "I know they're handmade in Mexico. Each pair is made to order. Maybe we could find out who he is by tracing the shoe."

I raised my hands to encompass the entire group. "It all leads to Mexico or close to it. Ivy missing after a trip to Mexico, six other people never heard from again. Poison from a Coral Snake, mostly seen in Texas and Mexico, and a dart used by the ancients.

"I'd say those people, on the boat, or at least some of them are not dead. Whatever happened on that trip was horrible enough to keep them out of sight for the past ten years. I can't imagine what it could be."

Ryan walked closer to me. "Let's tackle it in the morning when our minds aren't numb from stress and lack of sleep. It's after four a.m. He glanced at Nathan. "Can we drop you at home or back at Amy's?"

Nathan slumped down in the chair behind him. "I'm staying here. I don't care what they say or how many men you have here. I won't leave Amy. I might not be able to see her, but I just can't leave. Could you go by her house and pick up The Digger. I'm sure he's scared. I quickly put him inside before we left. I need to be able to tell her he's safe when she asks."

Ryan sat beside him. "I wouldn't leave if it were Kate in that bed. Do you want me to stay with you?"

He looked up at Ryan "No, the men you sent'll be here any minute. Just take care of the dog."

I leaned down and gave him a one-armed hug and a light kiss on the cheek. "Don't worry about the dog. We'll take care of him."

The scene at Amy's house sent a chill through me. A CSI team roamed about with cameras and test kits. Crime tape stretched around the trees and the house. Digger barked a *somebody save me* bark from inside.

CHAPTER 4

Ryan's phone rang mid-morning. Digger and Chili had been outside to potty and both burrowed back under the blankets where they had slept all night. I could tell from Ryan's end of the conversation it was Nathan. "That's good news. Have they taken her off the ventilator? Sure, we'll be there within the hour. Nathan? It's all going to be alright."

I had already turned on my side to face him. "So, I take it Amy is awake?"

"Yes, but she can't talk because of the breathing tube. He gave her something to write on. She wrote, *"I'm hungry."*

I responded with something between a sob and a laugh. I'd call it relief. "That's *so* Amy. I love that woman."

He leaned over and pulled me close. "I know you do, so do I. We'd better shower and head that way."

As much as I loved to take my shower with Ryan, I fed the dogs and set out the coffee pods and cream instead. By the time I headed upstairs, he was on his way outside to sit with them and drink a cup of coffee while I showered and dressed.

We were both allowed to see Amy. She looked flushed and tired. The spot where the barb struck her looked swollen and bruised. They announced they would remove the breathing apparatus after lunch.

I pulled one of the two chairs in the room up next to the bed. "We all need to talk. None of us is safe. If someone attacked Amy because of this... this mystery, they'll be after the rest of us too. The sooner we can track Ivy's movements for the past ten years, the better off we'll be."

Ryan stepped closer. "I'll keep two men on duty to guard each of us until we get some insight. Seven people don't fall off the face of the earth without someone seeing something. It's difficult to speculate about what happened since we don't have a single fact."

Nathan raised a hand in protest. "I don't need a bodyguard."

Ryan took a boss-like tone. "Yes, you do. I don't want one either, but there are four of us. We didn't expect any of this, but since it happened, we need to be prepared."

I reached for Amy's hand and squeezed it. "Obviously Coral Snakes are nothing to ignore. I have a couple of ideas. We need to find out all we can about the trip the Tucker's took. Read all the newspaper articles about the family, the Captain, and his wife as we can. Someone should probably go to Chicago and talk to the neighbors. People usually remember a family if something tragic happened to them."

Amy began to write and held up her message. It read *nobody had better go anywhere without me!*

It was the first time any of us had smiled together for three days.

I stayed with Amy while Ryan and two of his men took Nathan home to shower. There were more guards outside the room. I thought it might be a little much, but I didn't intend to voice my opinion.

Amy drifted in and out of sleep. The times she woke up I assured her Digger was happy and we would get her anything she wanted to eat as soon as the doctor freed her of the tubes.

When she slept, I took notes as to what we needed to do and in what order. By the time the guys came back, I had filled two complete pages and fallen asleep in my chair.

Ryan said, "It occurred to me,if someone is following us, they now know where we all live. Maybe it would be best if you and Amy," he nodded toward Nathan, "moved into the maid's quarters off the kitchen so we aren't so spread out."

Amy held up a sign. *"Maid's quarters?"*

I laughed. "We didn't know what to call it. It's not a guest room. No one would stick a guest room off the kitchen and the laundry room. It's twice the size of any of the other bedrooms in the house, including the master. There are two huge closets and a bathroom nicer than ours. It might have once been a mother-in-law or nanny's room, but I really like Maid's Quarters best."

We laughed again. Nathan looked at Amy for an answer. She shook her head *yes*. So much for being alone in the house during the first week of our vacation. I preferred it to the worry we would face if we were spread out all over the city.

We sprung Amy from the hospital the next morning. She insisted she go to her house with Nathan to pick out what she wanted to bring to our place. Ryan sent two men along with them plus the three who had watched the neighborhood since the assault.

Once they were settled in their new *home away from home*, I plopped down on the loveseat. Nathan and Ryan enjoyed a beer on the deck while they watched the dogs play. Amy wanted water. Her throat hurt. Her voice sounded hoarse and scratchy. "Doctor Sanchez said I could travel in a week, after one more blood test. Hopefully, you won't run off without me."

Ryan and Nathan came in. I picked up my glass and tipped it toward her. "We want to stick together. You couldn't shake us if you wanted to."

The doorbell rang. Ryan went to answer it. He came back with a box of papers. "Jacob dug up information on the Tucker family. I thought we might be able to learn something about them while Amy recuperates."

Ryan looked from one of us to another. "I've been reading about blow darts and snake venom. If he's good at it, and had a blow gun he could kill any one of us from fifty yards. For the next few days, we need to search different databases and see what we turn up. Next week, we will head for Chicago. If the four of us stay close to one another, not only can we solve this, but we can watch each other's backs."

"What about Digger and Chili?" she asked.

Nathan put his hand on her leg. "That's the big question. We don't know this man. We have no idea what he might do or if he would hurt one of the dogs."

Ryan took over. "Nathan and I talked about it outside. At first we thought we should take them with us. Then we decided, if you agree, we'll leave them here with some of the men. I have at least a dozen who are dog lovers. You two can interview them if you like and tell them exactly what you want them to do. I will send as many as you feel comfortable with. If you say two then two, if you ladies say ten, then we'll have ten. We're going to electrify the top of the fence so no one can climb it. I'll have cameras on any tree big enough for him to climb and shoot the dogs, or my men. I think it's the best answer.

"Jacob said he could rig cameras to work with your phones so you can look in on them anytime you want. He called it a *doggy cam*.

Amy nor I said anything. All Ryan had told me was he wanted to leave the dogs home with guards. When I heard the entire plan I thought it was excessive; over the top. In reality, it was Ryan being Ryan. He knew how much the furbabies meant to us. Amy stood and stretched. "I love my Digger, but even I think it's a little much. I would be happy with two men inside and two outside with the electric fence and cameras. What about you, Kate?"

"I'm fine with it so long as the dogs can sleep with the guys and they will escort them out every time they need to go. They can't go out alone."

"Okay, it's settled then. I'll get Jacob on the camera set up and Nathan will pick the dog lovers. He knows the men better than I do. People are always more reserved around the boss."

We went to our rooms early. Nathan hadn't slept much the last two days, Amy said she still harbored the after-effects of the antihistamines. I went over and gave her a hug. "Don't ever scare me that badly again."

"I don't know if we're even yet. I wasn't kidnapped by the Mafia and stayed missing for over a week."

"Touché."

CHAPTER 5

I felt a pressure on the bed and opened my eyes. Ryan sat on the side. "It's about time you woke up. Amy, Nathan, and I had breakfast and are on our second cup of coffee."

I looked over at the bedside table. "It's only eight o'clock. Why's everyone up so early?"

"I'm up to make the arrangements for all of the things we talked about last night. Amy's up because of nerves and a drug hangover. Nathan got up with her because he's worried about her. I know how he feels. There's nothing worse than thinking the one you love is in danger."

He leaned over and kissed me. I felt cold and empty when he moved away. "I'll be down in a few. I'm going to shower. Are there any bagels and cream cheese left?"

"There are. I know my woman. I would swim the ocean and back to keep your bagels stocked." He kissed me lightly as I walked by him on my way to the bathroom.

I finished in the shower and took my towel to wipe the bathroom mirror. My hair was a mess. I grew up with nicknames such as red, fire head, and Anne. I tried to wear my hair short, but it only became curlier and curlier until it turned into a huge afro I couldn't get a comb or brush through.

In seventh grade I learned the longer I let it grow the more the weight of it pulled out some of the curl. I wore it pulled back and lassoed it with a scrunchy to tame it.

I picked my favorite jeans and Cardinal tee shirt from my closet. Before I lived with Ryan, I left most of my clothes piled on the closet floor. I had a constant struggle with myself to hang them up or put them in the hamper. I couldn't keep it up for any length of time. I scolded myself as I dressed.

"Hi. How's the coffee?" Everyone knew I meant latte. A blueberry bagel with cream cheese and a tall latte had been a breakfast Amy and I ate every morning since the day we opened the office— seven years earlier.

Nathan handed me a cup of the hot liquid. "The bagels and the other stuff are on the table outside."

We didn't see much of one another for the next few hours. Ryan left for his office, the rest of us split the research Jacob sent over and went our separate ways to read. Nathan took his to the hammock under a giant oak in the backyard. Amy stretched out on the love seat with her feet on the ottoman. I sat on the couch with my legs tucked under me. Both dogs snuggled together on the other end.

We all took notes so we could put our information together later. I found it interesting reading—*the Tucker children were high achievers.*

Amy looked up. "This article says, *they had the trip planned down to the minutest detail. They hired a Captain and his wife who would serve as a mate."*

Nathan came in. "The FBI has never closed the case. They say the wreckage of the boat proves foul play. Makes you wonder if the entire family has been in hiding and whoever wanted them dead, found Ivy."

Amy chimed in again. "There are three feature stories about the family and the trip. One was when the authorities found pieces of the boat, the second was at the one-year anniversary of the finding of the ship and the last one, a week ago, on the ten-year anniversary."

I smiled. "Good luck for us. It'll be fresh in everyone's mind. It's as if I know the Tuckers already. The book of information I have has at least a hundred pictures of the family. Such a shame. I hope we can solve the mystery."

Ryan came back and joined in. "You do realize the FBI, the Illinois authorities, the authorities of Mexico, California, and the Coast Guard have not been able to figure out what happened to the boat and the family?"

Amy went to the kitchen where Nathan had begun to make breakfast. My brother-in-law, Tony, was a chef, but to have two men in the house with us who liked to cook was heaven. She looked back over her shoulder and answered Ryan. "They aren't us. We are fresh eyes and they don't know Ivy survived all those years. Well, they might know by now."

"Since Chicago is only five hours, I thought we would drive. I am taking one of the Explorers from the company. It happens to have bulletproof glass. I don't think anyone will try to shoot us, but I think I would prefer it to dying from a dose of snake venom."

The doorbell rang. I moved toward it. Ryan stopped me. "Don't answer that. My men are out there. They know to call or radio before they come in. Something's wrong."

Nathan came out of the kitchen area and walked to the patio door. To the left of it, the monitors to the cameras Ryan had installed were visible. "I have a funny feeling. I see no one. None of the men are visible. I'll call Danny."

By then we all stood around him and peered at the monitors. They showed the chair by the front door, the one outside the back gate, and scanned the street. We could see the SUV was gone. "Danny doesn't answer. I'll try one of the others."

Ryan walked over to the table and picked up his cell phone. "While you do that, I'll check with Jacob at the office and see what he has on the larger monitor."

I could tell by the look they had on their faces the news had not been good. Nathan spoke first. "Danny, Mike, John, Phil, and Ray— none of them answer."

Ryan added. "Jacob wasn't at the monitors. He had gone to another room to set the guys up to start the background checks."

Amy put her hands to her face. "I'm so sorry. We should have done our own work."

"No," Ryan said," there's nothing on his monitor either and the car has not made a pass around the house for over an hour. He could tell by the time stamp."

I had been quiet, turning my head from speaker to speaker in order to keep up with the conversation. "So, surely someone didn't overpower four strong men and a guy in an SUV so he could ring the doorbell."

Ryan went to the refrigerator, reached on top and retrieved his gun. Nathan did the same. "Depends on who it is and what he's delivering, whatever the case may be. Amy, I know you're still weak. Maybe you should sit this one out."

"Not on your life," she answered. "Should we call Roger and have him send a patrol car?"

Ryan walked toward the patio door. "We can handle this. I need to know what happened to my men. They are not easily fooled or overtaken." He took a stick camera and held it clear of the top of the fence and turned it in all directions. "There's nothing. No movement of any kind. I hate to do it but alert Roger. After what happened to Amy, I don't want to go out or send anyone into danger without at least an inkling of what happened out there."

I made the call but bypassed 911 and called Roger's cell phone. After I explained the situation, I added, "Please, no sirens!"

He agreed.

A half an hour had passed and still no word from our detective. We all paced, lost in our own thoughts. We waited an hour before I called again. "What's going on? Did you send someone?"

I had the speaker on. "Yes, I did. Four men are down, and the car and driver are nowhere to be found. I thought it best to get the men medical attention. I'm not sure what's in the package on the porch. I have the bomb squad on its way. Don't open the front door."

Ryan leaned in so he could talk. "What is wrong with the men?"

"Hard to tell at this point, three of them are unconscious with not a mark on any of them. The fourth looks like he did several rounds with a professional fighter. He's awake, but in too much pain to talk."

"Nathan and I are coming out. I'll try to keep Kate and Amy inside, but I don't guarantee it. We are exiting by the patio gate. Don't shoot us."

"Listen you guys, if any of you come out, it's against my order. Look at all the precautions we took to keep these people away from you and it didn't seem to do any good. The way you could help me most is to get me a description of the missing car and driver, and the license plate number."

Ryan put his hand up. "Here's the way I see it. My men are hurt, maybe fatally. I'm going out to see what I can do. I would like for the rest of you to stay put, but I made my decision and you have a right to make yours. Amy, I think you should stay in. I'm not sure your body could take anymore at this point."

Nathan walked over and hugged her. "I love you Amy. Please stay out of this until you are stronger. I promise we'll let you know every little thing that goes on. I'll get your side arm in case you have a problem in here. Kate, are you armed? If so, let's go."

Amy didn't put up a fight. Her eyes were swollen, her cheeks sunken, and her movements slow. If I had to guess, I'd say she wanted to stay inside.

Outside looked like a raid. The swat team roamed around in full riot gear and carried assault rifles. They covered every inch of the property, shoulder to shoulder the way I had seen search teams do when they looked for a missing person.

Four ambulances and their crews tended the men. Ryan went from one to the next, shook his head and moved on. His shoulders sagged, he looked ten years older. When he saw me, he came to me with outstretched arms. We held on to one another for a long moment.

"What happened to them," I asked.

"They were poisoned with something. None of the medical personnel here think it was snake venom."

"How do they know?"

"Whoever did this rendered them incapacitated with a dart in the neck. Probably after they were all down, he injected them with something. There is a puncture wound on the back of the neck and another in the bend of their arm. The wound on the neck, if snake venom would be enough to kill them, the extra injection would not have been needed."

"What has that dead girl gotten us into? I am so sorry, Ryan."

"None of us are at fault. Who would expect a dead body on their porch in the first place? The bomb squad is here; let's go see what's in the box."

Nathan reached the porch at the same time we did. He had come from the house. I assume he either checked on Amy or updated her on the activities outside.

The bomb squad had a man dressed in a blast-proof suit. In front of him, he pushed a box on wheels. He controlled it with a gadget in his hands. He warned us to move back away from the box. We did, with the help of the swat team who had set up a perimeter with their backs to us. Ten minutes later the man declared, "It is not a bomb. It looks like a piece of wood. He carefully opened it while we all watched through the arms of our guards. "Yes, it's a piece of wood, it has writing on it. You people involved can see it, but don't touch it. No telling what it might have on it, poison, or maybe even a fingerprint."

Nathan stood as close as he could. "Looks like Spanish. Anyone know what it says?"

My heart sank. "I do. It says Iguana Veloz. It means Speedy Iguana, the name of the boat the Tucker's were on when they disappeared. "I read the entire sign out loud, *Speedy Iguana, Smith River, California.* I think someone is trying to tell us something. I wish we knew who it was, another person from the Tucker family, or maybe the Captain or his wife."

"Or maybe a stranger," Amy said from where she now stood in the doorway.

CHAPTER 6

The tactical team left. Ryan's men were on their way to the hospital, we went inside. Roger followed. "I guess what happened on the Tucker's trip isn't what everyone has thought all these years. There's at least one more person who survived other than Ivy. Why that person is coming out in public after all this time is perplexing."

I offered Roger a seat and a cup of coffee. "My theory is that sometime during the trip, Ivy witnessed a crime. She decided to share what she knew with you. This other person on the boat found out and killed her before she could tell her story. The person in question doesn't know how long we had been in contact with the girl. Whatever it was, it must have been horrendous for him or her to be willing to kill indiscriminately to keep the secret."

Ryan, who sat on the arm of the couch while we talked, stood. "I have every intention of finding the person who harmed or potentially killed my employees. Right now, you will have to excuse me. I need to notify their families and fill them in on what happened. I have three more men coming to escort me, although I have no idea why. It didn't work last time."

Roger turned to leave. "You know as well as I do, Ryan. If someone wants to get to you, they will. Locks and keys only keep honest people honest."

"Not very encouraging, Roger," I said.

Ryan and Roger left at the same time, headed to the same place, the hospital.

Ryan called a few hours later, he sounded tired. "This time he used rattle snake venom. The small wound on the neck was a dart filled with it. The doctor said it was not good they were bitten, so to speak, in the neck. The main thing is to keep them from moving around too much. The more they move the more damage it can do. They should be alright. Whoever this person is, he must have a powerful secret to keep."

"Have they found your driver?"

"No, Ray and the SUV are still missing. They're looking. I'm putting a GPS tracking device on every vehicle as soon as possible. Is Nathan close?"

"Sure, he's right here." I handed him the phone and went to tell Amy the latest. She had gone to take a nap earlier.

Nathan came to the doorway. Whatever he needed to say, he didn't want to say it. "We know this will be annoying, but Ryan wants four of our guys in the house. He believes, at least, we'll all be safe in here. They're stopping for food and anything else we might want. They'll each call from the curb and then at the door. They'll have a password for curb and another for the porch. If any one of them doesn't know the passwords, *shoot him*. I can only hope he wasn't serious about the last part."

An hour later all four men were in the house and we had enough food and beverages for a month. Nathan introduced them. Their names were Keith, Darren, Bobby, and Shorty— who stood at least six-feet-eight.

All this time the dogs were ignored. Nathan took them on short trips to the backyard for potty breaks. They were restless and moved from Amy to me, and back every five minutes.

A young man, who had been introduced as Bobby, walked over to pet Chili. She ran as fast as she could to the patio door and hid behind the curtain. I'd never seen her so skittish. Bobby followed her and spoke softly. He sat on the floor next to her. "I know who you are. You're Chili. I think we should be friends. I'm one of the people who will watch you while Miss Nash solves this case."

Chili took a tiny step toward him as he held out a treat to her. She came out from her hiding place, grabbed the morsel and ran back. "Are you playing hard to get?" Bobby asked her. Not to be left out, Digger walked behind the man and wagged his tail. "You must be Digger. Are you going to run from me also?" The Yorkie stood his ground, took a treat, and ran back to Amy. She looked up at Nathan. "Do you think it will be okay to leave them? Things haven't gone too well so far?"

"Yes, they'll be fine. Ryan sets up security systems, it's his business. He admits he underestimated the tenacity of whoever we're dealing with. He said he won't do it a second time. Before you leave, this house and grounds will be so secure; it would be easier to get into the US Mint."

A huge thud came from outside the front door. Shorty took a convex mirror and surveyed the area. "It's Ray. Sounds like someone dumped him on the porch. Nathan, can we go after him?"

Nathan took the mirror away from Shorty and looked for himself. "I can't tell if he's okay or not. Kate, we're going out to get him. Want to call 911 in case he's hurt?"

With that, they were out the door and back in a flash with Ray. He didn't look too bad. "Ray, can you hear me?"

"Yes, he didn't hurt me; he just wanted to send a message to Kate Nash and her friends who found Ivy Tucker. His exact words were—*Let the dead rest peacefully. Don't dredge up things that don't concern you. I have made it abundantly clear I am serious. Go back to your own lives and I will return to my watery grave.* Once he was sure I would give you the message with the reverence it deserved, he brought me here and dropped me off. The thud you heard was a large rock."

I looked around the room. "Doesn't it make you believe whoever it is was on the boat and supposed dead? The part... *I will return to my watery grave.*"

Amy canceled the 911 call and I spoke to Ryan. "Ray's here. The man gave him a message for us and dropped him off. They came here in a taxi. Ray said the company car is in the Mississippi River, and the man is scary. How are things there?" I hung up. "Ryan will be home in a little while. Ray, are you hungry?"

"Yes, Ma'am."

"Oh my, call me Kate. I have a feeling we're all going to be very good friends before this is over."

While all of this went on, Chili and Digger sat back and waited. Once we were settled, both dogs jumped up on Bobby's lap. He and Keith took them out and walked around the backyard.

The sleeping arrangements reminded me of dorm living at Northwestern. There were bodies everywhere. One man sat by the patio door, another by the back door and one by the front. The fourth man slept in the downstairs guest room. Ryan and I went to our room.

I took a shower. Ryan changed into lounging pants and a tee shirt and lay stretched out on the bed. He had his arms folded behind his head and his head on the pillow. "A penny for your thoughts."

I don't think they are worth more. My theory is one of them murdered all the rest, somehow, Ivy survived, and the killer found out and killed her too. He's trying to stop us so no one will find out what really happened on the boat."

I towel dried my hair, gathered it low on my neck and held it in place with a blue ribbon. "I agree, any ideas what to do next?"

"I have a few. We need to go to Chicago, find out if the Tuckers were the people they appeared to be in the articles we've read. Sometimes, friends and relatives have experiences and facts not fit for the news."

He patted the bed next to him and turned toward my side. "I'm too tired to give it anymore thought tonight. The worry and stress have wiped me out."

"Okay, can we go over one more thing before we turn in?" I pulled back the covers and crawled in. I had to maneuver my legs around Chili, who had already burrowed to the bottom of the bed. I didn't wait for him to answer. "What kind of description did Ray give you?"

"He said the guy had on a disguise, long blond wig, bushy eyebrows, and ill-fitting clothes. The only thing he didn't try to hide was that he was left-handed. He was tall, slim, and the skin he didn't have covered was deeply tanned."

I reached over to the bedside table to turn off the lamp. When I turned back, Ryan was sound asleep. I leaned over, kissed him on the cheek, and snuggled in with him and the dog.

I didn't expect to sleep with the events of the day swirling around inside my head, but I did. I dreamed of snakes, natives with blow darts, and big boats.

CHAPTER 7

There were no more incidents before we left for Chicago. We discussed safety. "Amy and I have been in some tight situations and have always been okay. If we show up at their friends and neighbors with an army, who will talk to us?"

"I have to agree," said Ryan, "at least we should stay in pairs."

We all agreed.

The next morning we left the dogs and the house in the capable hands of Shorty and Bobby. I wore what I considered my uniform. A white blouse, tailored slacks, a blazer to cover my Glock 44, and spike heels. I wore heels everywhere.

Amy wore practically the same thing, except for the heels. At five-feet-ten, she didn't need them.

Nathan drove first. We stopped by the Starbuck's on the University Loop and had breakfast. Amy and I had our usual. Nathan lathered a bagel with cream cheese. "This won't hold me for long. Ryan and I get to pick where we stop for lunch. I can't do my best work if I'm hungry."

Amy playfully kidded him. "We *will* allow you to eat something more than a bagel. They have other items you might like."

Nathan and Ryan walked to the front to buy more food. I watched them. Ryan was the shorter of the two, with a wrestler's body. His pants fit tight at the thighs, not because of fat, but muscle. He had broad shoulders accented by the tangerine polo shirt he wore. Nathan's body resembled a basketball player's, tall and lean. He filled out his clothes equally well.

My preoccupation kept me from seeing a man until he fell into our table, stumbled and knocked it a few feet from where it sat. Amy jumped first. "Stop where you are. Don't take another step or I'll shoot."

In one fluid motion I stood and stepped behind him. He had his hands in the air. "Whoa, ladies. I didn't mean to upset your breakfast." He put his arms down and reached toward his pocket.

I jabbed my Glock into his back. "I wouldn't move if I were you."

The men were back. One stood on each side of him. He turned toward Ryan. "Can you settle these women down? I didn't mean anything."

Ryan turned his face away from the man and took a step back. "Did you drink your breakfast, fella?"

The man became belligerent. "Who do you people think you are? I'm going to have you arrested."

About then a cop walked in. "I got a call about a disturbance here."

The barista must have called. She pointed in our direction.

He came toward us and drew his gun, most likely because Amy and I stood in a, move and I'll shoot, stance, guns pointed at the guy from front and back. "Let's all settle down. Ladies, put your weapons on the floor."

We did.

"Kick them over to me."

We did.

"What happened here?"

Amy took a step toward the officer. "I might have overreacted. I was assaulted two weeks ago and they haven't caught the perp. I'm a bit jumpy."

"I need to see your permits for these weapons."

I reached in my back pocket, retrieved my PI license, and gun permit.

"Mrs. Nash. Sorry, I've never seen you in person. Do you want me to call Captain Simon?"

I looked at his name badge. "No Officer Jenkins. It won't be necessary. I think this was an accident. We jumped too soon."

He looked at the man in the center of the controversy. "Would you like to tell me what happened?"

The man pulled up a chair and sat. I guessed he didn't want the cop to see how drunk he was. "My wife and I had a fight. I went out last night and drank too much. I came here to sit, have coffee, and think. I was on my way for a refill when I side-stepped and knocked into these folks' table." He looked from one of us to the other with a scowl on his face. It sent a chill down my back.

The officer looked at us. "You can pick up your weapons, and finish your breakfast. I'll make a report on Mr.— what is your name, sir?"

They went to the back of the coffee shop. We could hear the calm voice of the officer and the agitated voice of the man.

No one had an appetite after the incident. We waited. A few minutes later, the officer came back. "He has had too much to drink, but I have no reason to arrest him. He isn't driving or causing trouble."

Says he'll walk around the Loop and get sober before he goes home. You folks are free to go," He stuck out his hand and shook each one of ours.

As we walked to the car, Ryan began to laugh. "Mrs. Nash, I've never gotten to meet you in person. I thought he was going to kiss your ring."

Amy chimed in. "Because I was with Mrs. Nash, I didn't have to show my ID."

"Neither did we."

We joked all the way to the car. The laughter stopped when we saw it. All four tires were flat, there was a note on the windshield, in what appeared to be shoe polish. *Does someone else have to die to get your attention?*

Ryan called his office and had them bring another SUV. I called Roger and told him what happened. He didn't sound happy. "Kate, maybe you should rethink your plan to investigate this yourself. The FBI, Federal Ministerial Police of Mexico, Coast Guard, and at least five local agencies are trying to solve it. This guy's serious. Maybe the man in the coffee shop was a decoy?"

"Ryan and Nathan ran back to the store to question him. He was nowhere in sight."

"You guys want to come down and visit with an artist?"

"Maybe later. Right now we need to get going."

"Don't touch that car until my crew gets there."

The four of us sat on the curb. The cops were prompt as were Ryan's men who brought a white Ford Explorer and transferred our belongings from the defunct car.

We had begun our trip at eight, afternoon approached evening before we were on the road again.

"Do you think it could have been the drunk guy in Starbucks?" I asked.

Ryan sat beside me in the back seat. "I don't understand how someone could have vandalized the car on a busy street without anyone noticing."

Nathan looked into the rearview mirror. "Hate to bring this up, but I'm hungry."

Amy had an idea. "Let's go through a drive-in, order the food, stop at a rest stop and have a picnic so the car is in our sight."

We followed Amy's plan and arrived at The Ritz-Carlton after midnight. Ryan had rented a two bedroom apartment with a panoramic view of Lake Michigan.

The car sat in valet parking under lock and key.

Our plan included a trip to Northwestern Memorial Hospital, the old neighborhood where the Tuckers lived, and the travel agency we knew helped them plan the trip.

We had room service bring breakfast to avoid any more mishaps. Ryan rented a pickup truck and a car so we could leave the SUV where it sat.

Amy and Nathan left for the hospital. We headed to meet the neighbors.

We went to the house listed on the information we had. It looked lived in. The lawn was shaggy and hadn't been trimmed in the recent past. A new Volvo sat in the driveway with a flat tire.

We stopped at the house next door to the old Tucker home. A middle-aged woman answered the door. "Hi, my name is Kate Nash, I'm a private investigator." I showed my license and gave her a card. "This is my associate, Ryan Meade."

"May I help you with something?"

"We hope so. Are you Mrs. Caulfield?"

"Yes, how can I help you?"

I took a deep breath and began. "There has been new information in the case of the missing Tucker family. We were hoping you could give us some insight into them."

She stepped outside and looked around the neighborhood. She pointed to the truck parked on the street. "It that your truck?"

Ryan looked at me and nodded to her. "Is there a problem?"

She stepped back out of the doorway.

"Ivy Tucker was found dead two weeks ago in St. Louis," I said.

"It can't be. Please, come in." She stepped aside and made room for us to pass. "May I get you a drink?"

Ryan smiled. "No, Mrs. Caulfield, that won't be necessary."

"I insist." We followed her to a small kitchen in the back of the house. "Even after all of these years, I have never been able to get those poor people off my mind. Such a horrible accident."

A coffee pot sat on an old fashioned blue tile counter. I scanned the room. It was a throwback to the ninety's. Coffee cups were hung on hooks under the cabinet. I hadn't seen it done for years. My heart pitter-pattered. My mom stored hers the same way in Florida. I was sure I didn't have another emotion to waste on her, but maybe I did.

She placed the cups in front of us along with a spoon, and pushed a cream pitcher and sugar dish our way. As she talked, she folded up the newspaper she must have been reading when we interrupted her morning. She turned the paper upside down so we could not see the subject of her reading. Once she had it the way she wanted, she slipped it onto her lap. "I don't know how familiar you are with the story of the Tuckers. They left here ten years ago and were somehow lost in the Sea of California and never seen or heard from again. It must be a case of mistaken identity. Ivy is dead, is this someone's idea of a cruel joke?"

"I know it comes as a shock to you, but somehow Ivy survived. No one knows how she did or where she has been. They positively identified her from fingerprints her parents had taken when she was young. The reason we are here is to talk to you about the family."

"It is hard to wrap my head around this news. Do

you think the rest of them survived?"

"No. There has been a man around. His actions and disruptions leads us to believe the rest are dead and he doesn't want any investigation into the accident if that is what it was."

She stared at me with eyes so hard I wanted to shrink; they brimmed with tears. Her facial expression didn't soften."I wonder where she was? Three years ago, the authorities went through the horrible ritual of having them all declared dead. Sharon's brother came, cleaned out the rest of the house, put it up for sale, and left. I assume he received the life insurance monies and all the rest."

"What do you mean by *all the rest*?"

The woman crossed her legs, picked up her coffee, but never took a sip of the liquid inside. "Oh my. There was Sharon's BMW and her beautiful jewelry. He had a Land Rover, they had a boat. The collection of Mexican Art they had in their home had been valued at several hundred thousand dollars. They sometimes loaned pieces to museums."

"What happened to their belongings?" I asked.

"A man came, said he was her brother from Mexico. I called the police, but the man had papers, deeds, records of all types and a will signed by both doctors."

Ryan hadn't said anything up until then. "So did the furnishings and personal items stay in the house for seven years until they were declared dead?"

"No, men in large trucks came and packed it all. An FBI agent dropped by and said the man was the Executer of the will and everything would go into storage until the Tuckers were found, or seven years passed, whichever came first."

"Do you know what her brother's name was?"

She walked over to a bulletin board on the other side of the room. "I don't remember off hand, but I wrote it down. I'm not sure why. It had nothing to do with me." She went through the items on the board. After a few minutes, she turned around with a note in her hand. "Here it is—Alberto Flores, La Paz, Mexico. He didn't give me a street address. He said the loss of so much family made him so sad, he never wanted to come here again."

Ryan glanced at me and back at our hostess. "So Dr. Tucker was Hispanic?"

"Yes, thus the big trip so she could show the children and her husband where she was raised and her beautiful homeland. All of them were bilingual. The children spoke Spanish at home and English when they were out."

Ryan continued. "Did you ever sense the Tuckers had any family or marriage problems?"

She became increasingly more upset. "Heavens no. All three children came here after school for years. They were a happy, normal, loving family."

"Are there any other neighbors we should speak to who knew the Tuckers well?" I asked.

"No, we have made a cycle in the past ten years. Most of these homes are occupied by executives who get transferred every few years. The only other people were the Cramers, Matthew, and June. June died a few years ago and Matthew moved away without saying goodbye."

"We won't keep you any longer. I only have one

more question. Can you describe Alberto Flores?"

"It was a long time ago." She closed her eyes and I wondered if she did it to conjure up an image. "He was about five-feet-ten, dark hair, and eyes, and a deep tan. He didn't speak with an accent although the card he gave me indicated he lived in Mexico."

Ryan stood and pulled out my chair. "Thank you for all of the information. You were very helpful."

She walked us to the door. As we left she asked a question of her own. "How did Ivy die?"

"She died from a coral snake bite.".

She said nothing, closed the door and watched us through the living room window as we drove away.

CHAPTER 8

Our next stop was the travel agency listed as the Tucker's source of information. The lady at the counter said, "They were a lovely family. I didn't do much for them. They had the trip mapped down to the tiniest detail. My only contribution was to provide the name of a seaworthy boat rental in Smith River."

"Do you know if they were going to hire a captain or any other help for the trip?" I asked.

She laughed and said, "You'll probably think this is crazy after all these years, but I remember the captain's name. It was Upton Bridges. It's not a name you hear every day and it stuck with me all these years."

Ryan wrote the name down in his notepad. "Do you remember anything else about the trip?"

"Only that when the FBI was here to investigate, they gave me another name for the captain. They said a sailor and his wife were both hired. The Agent said the woman was hired to do the cooking. I know it isn't true. There is no way Dr. Sharon would take someone along to cook. She was excited about the family cooking together on the boat. She had all the meals planned.

"They had to have had a very good reason to go with another captain and bring on a mate. They were going to stay gone for three full months. Captain Bridges took the job because he was about to retire and he didn't care how long the trip."

"Did you ever Google Bridges to see what he looked like?"

"I did. I could describe him to you but if I could find him, so could you."

I handed the woman my card. "If you think of anything else, no matter how small, would you please call me?"

"Yes, but what is this about? Are you writing a story or something?"

"Actually, we found Ivy Tucker dead on our front porch two weeks ago and we are going to find out what happened to her."

Both of the travel agents' hands went to their face. "How horrible. I wonder where she was for over ten years? Do you think any of the rest of them are alive?"

"I'm afraid we don't know much. But it is a puzzle we intend to solve. Thanks for your help."

At six o'clock we met Amy and Nathan in the room. Ryan loosened his tie. "Anyone hungry? I'll treat us to dinner at the Torali. It's right here in the hotel. We can exchange information over some good food and a bottle of wine."

"I'm game. Do I need a jacket?" Nathan asked.

"No. It's casual. The food is good and Kate and I didn't stop to eat today."

Amy walked over and put her hand on the door as if she was ready to go. "We didn't either."

The restaurant encompassed the entire top floor of the hotel. A little less than half of it was open air. A bar separated the inside from the outside. We chose to sit in a back corner where we had a complete view of the city and the rest of the cafe including the alfresco tables and the bar.

For an appetizer we ordered fried calamari with sweet cherry peppers and marinara sauce. We munched on the octopus as we studied the menu. The waiter recommended the Flat Iron Wagyu steak to Ryan. Amy and I chose King salmon, with romanesco and capers.

Nathan handed me the wine list. "Do you have a favorite?"

Amy smiled at him. "I like a Pinot Noir, so does Kate."

Ryan picked a Cabernet to complement their steaks. No one said anything until the food arrived and Ryan had finished the ritual of tasting the wine.

I began to eat my salad. "We found out a little about the Tuckers from their neighbor. She made them sound like saints. She did say no one came to the house until after they were declared dead, except for the FBI who packed their belongings and put them in storage. Once they were missing seven years. I find that strange. At that time, Sharon's brother flew in from Mexico, cleaned out the house, put it up for sale and she thinks he also was heir to any money they had."

Amy sat her wine glass on the table. "Same thing at the hospital. Wonderful, sweet, hardworking and dedicated doctors, Sharon went to UNAM, short for Universidad Nacional Autonoma de Mexico, and Harvard Medical School. We heard the word genius more than once today when her name came up.

"Eric was a pediatrician. They met at Harvard. Every chance they had to spend together, they did. Two different people told us as they passed one another in the hall, they would touch each other's hands."

Nathan took a small notebook from his pocket and opened it. "The three kids, Dallas, Max, and Ivy were their lives. Nothing bad there. Nothing."

Ryan added. "The most significant fact we heard was her brother's name, Alberto Flores and he lives in La Paz. She described him. He fits into the parameters of what we know of our stranger."

Dinner relaxed me. We talked and laughed and shared another glass of wine. As we were about to leave, the waiter brought four different desserts to our table. "These were sent to your table by the gentleman sitting outside at the bar." He looked up and out. "He isn't there any longer."

I looked at the opulent plates he sat on the table. "How did the gentleman pay for these? Did he use a credit card?"

"No miss, I went to the bar to get the wine for you and he paid cash for the food and a generous tip. He asked me to bring these to you before you paid your check."

"Can you describe him?"

"Yes, medium height, black hair, and dark eyes. I'm sorry if I did something wrong, ma'am. He spoke as if he knew you."

Amy pushed the tray to the center of the table. "No, you did nothing wrong. We would have liked to say hello and thank our friend, that's all."

Ryan looked up at the waiter. "Please bill this to room 2724."

"Yes, sir. You don't want the pastries?"

"No, we're all too full. Please give them to the staff."

During the ride downstairs to our rooms, no one said a word. The elevator door opened, nobody moved. On my signal, Ryan and Nathan stepped out into the hall and looked around. Amy and I followed. I didn't let go of the breath I held until we were in the room and the door locked behind us.

We cleared the rooms police style, guns drawn, closets, bathrooms, living room, and kitchen. Nothing seemed out of place.

I took off my jacket, gun holster, and shoes before I plopped on the couch. "He's here. It's spooky. The description from the waiter and the next door neighbor are enough alike to make me think it is the same person."

Ryan sat next to me. "I wonder if the man who went to the Tucker home three years ago and settled the estate was Doctor Tucker's brother."

Amy walked in from the kitchen. "I have my doubts. We've read volumes of information on them. His parents are deceased. His brother lives abroad and his sister in a nun in Wisconsin. There's never been a mention of her having living relatives. She was an only child with parents who both died young. What do you think we should do next?"

"Get some sleep," Nathan said and followed his words with a yawn.

Amy perched on the arm of the love seat. "I say we talk to the FBI, although they don't always tell everything they know. I'll call first thing in the morning."

On his way to our room, Ryan stopped at the window. He turned toward us. "I had forgotten how beautiful the skyline is against the lake." We all joined him and picked out landmarks we had seen in photos all of our lives.

Nathan put his hand on the wall and leaned forward to look down the side of the hotel. "What do you think about this guy who dogs our every step?"

Amy went to stand beside him. He moved his hand off the window and put it around her. "I believe he's the key to this mystery. I know we haven't seen the end of him. Don't you wonder how he knew what hotel we booked, where we would have dinner, and what time?"

Ryan didn't move, he stared out the window. I put my hands on his back. "At first I thought he must have had listening and tracking devices on the car. Since we changed to rental cars, I'm lost."

Amy put her finger in front of her mouth in *a don't say another word* gesture.

I tapped Ryan to get his attention. Nathan had already begun a sweep of the rooms for a *bug*. We got more than we bargained for. A contraption hidden in the sprinkler, looked like it both listened to our conversations and videotaped our movements.

Ryan stood on a chair, pulled the device out and took a closer look. He handed it to Nathan who did the same. Nathan took it to the kitchen sink and ran hot water on it for a few minutes, then flushed it down the toilet in the bathroom. He came back into the room. "It's not a brand I'm familiar with. Anyone else recognize it?"

"The symbol on it was Chinese. Most of the stuff we use is from there. I took a picture of it and sent it to Jacob before you destroyed it. I don't think it was a professional grade. Jacob will track it down in the morning and let us know. I believe it's something you could buy online, maybe even on Amazon."

We searched but didn't find anything else. Another reason to make me think he was an amateur. Amy ushered us all into the bathroom. We closed the door, turned on the water in the shower, the sink, and flushed the toilet so no one could hear our conversation if we missed a listening device. "I say we change our story about Ivy's murder. Don't mention anything else we find out. Let's say it's time to go home, leave this to the authorities, and get back to our lives. If we do give out any information, let's make sure it's misleading."

Everyone gave a thumbs up and we went to our separate rooms. The desire for conversation or romance had been killed by the spy camera and bug we found.

The next morning before we went out to breakfast at IHOP, my phone rang. I didn't recognize the number and answered hesitantly. "Hello, Mrs. Caulfield." I shrugged my shoulders. "Slow down. Tell me again what happened. Really, what did he want? Did he threaten you? No, we don't have any information yet. We are going to the FBI tomorrow and then heading back to St. Louis. If anything else happens, Mrs. Caulfield, call me, and thank you."

"What was that about?" Ryan asked.

"Seems after we left, a man came to see her. He told her if she wanted to stay safe, she needed to forget anything and everything she knows about the Tucker family. He told her helping the nosey people would only get her hurt."

"Did she call the police?"

"No, she was afraid. He fits the description of the man who kidnapped Ray, and the man your guys saw near the house. She didn't recognize him as the man who claimed to be Dr. Tucker's brother."

"Interesting," Amy said. "Let's talk about it in the morning. My belly is full and my legs are tired." She headed toward their room. "Are you coming?" She called over her shoulder to Nathan.

Amy called it right, we'd had enough for one day.

The next morning we packed before we left for the café. Amy and Nathan agreed to go back to our room and watch as the bellman took our luggage to the foyer so no one could tamper with it.

The plan we devised split us up. Ryan and I were headed for the FBI office. An agent met us on the main floor, led us to a room, and left us there. I took a business card out of my back pocket and laid it on the table. Another agent came in. "I'm Agent DeFore, one of the men who originally investigated the Tucker case. How can I help you?"

"Will you open the case again now that Ivy Tucker was found dead in St. Louis?" I asked.

He tapped his fingers on a manila folder he brought in with him and put on the table in front of him. "In this case, I believe you have me at a disadvantage. Word about her death hasn't reached me yet. I don't think it has even been logged into the case files. What's your interest in this?" He looked down at my card.

"Miss Tucker was found dead on our front porch two weeks ago."

"Do you know how she was killed?"

"Yes, snake venom."

"Weird. You're more than welcome to look through the file. We most likely won't reopen the case. Once you have read it, you'll understand." He pushed the packet toward us and left the room.

I opened it and began to read. Ryan moved closer so he could see the documents as I took them out of the packet.

We had all the information they had except for the name of the boat rental location and name, the captain's and his wife's physical information.

Fifteen minutes later, the agent came back. I stood. "Thanks for letting us read this."

"Was it helpful?" he asked.

"No, but it was good to know our information is correct."

Ryan and I shook his hand and were escorted back to the lobby.

Amy and Nathan sat in the foyer having an ice tea and waiting for us.

Ryan said he would settle the bill while Nathan called for the car.

Ten minutes later, in a park, we stopped while the guys scanned for GPS trackers and listening devices.

The car had neither.

Amy asked, "Did you learn anything?"

I turned my body so I faced more toward the backseat. "The information we have on the family is spot on. I think the man who settled the estate is our attacker.

"Michael Mannes was or is the Captain's name. His new wife, Janis, went along on the trip as the cook. Michael Mannes has black hair, brown eyes, and is five-feet-ten. The only difference between him and our guy is the weight. Mannes weighed 195."

Amy leaned forward. "A person can change in ten years."

I turned back toward Ryan. "I think we should make a trip to Smith River, find the boat rental, and see what we can dig up about the captain and his wife,"

Amy reached forward from the back seat and put her hand on my shoulder. "I think the trip is a good idea, but I want to stay with the dogs. I don't like the idea of them being uprooted and with strangers."

Nathan gave her a hug. "I agree. We'll stay at the house with the animals. You two follow the path and find out what you can. I'm fairly sure we'll be fine. The man in question will be much more likely to follow you. We're no threat to him in St. Louis."

Ryan looked into the rearview mirror to look at Nathan. "I agree. I would feel better if we had a couple of men there. They don't have to be in the house. With the new lights, no one can move without giving themselves away."

We walked into the house and the dogs went wild. They ran from me to Amy to Ryan and Nathan and back again. This went on for a good ten minutes. I knew then, the decision for Amy and Nathan to stay at the house while we were gone was the best one.

CHAPTER 9

R yan and I flew to Crecent City on one of the company's planes with the hope it would be more difficult to track us if we used private transportation. At the rental counter in the airport, we chose an SUV and drove the fifteen miles to Smith River.

We found the boat rental with no problem. Iguana Boat Rentals stood out from the others. A twenty-foot full-color Iguana sign hung with giant hooks marked the entrance. The Tucker boat had the same insignia on the side, only much smaller.

I'd never been in a boat as large as the ones docked there. They all had Iguana in the name.

The owner, a British fellow in his sixties, remembered the Tuckers for two reasons, the tragic demise of an entire family and the loss of his boat.

When Ryan asked about the Captain, the gentleman frowned.

I noticed his look. "So you didn't like Michael Mannes?"

"No one did. He was an odd man. His first wife disappeared a few years before he went on the trip with the Tuckers. He told all of us she left him. We had no way of knowing and no one came looking for her. He just didn't mention her again."

Ryan stepped closer to the counter. "We heard he had a new wife."

"Oh, her. They were two peas in a pod. I suggested to Dr. Tucker they wait for Captain Bridges to return from a twelve-day tour. The tour he hosted ran into bad weather and they were forced to dock for three days.

They didn't want to wait. Said their trip was time sensitive because of the rain and winds in the Pacific. I told them it was less than a week, but they wouldn't hear of it. I'm not busy, would you like to sit and have a cold drink?" He pointed to one of the brightly painted tables in the room.

Ryan walked to a pop machine with the owner and helped carry the drinks. He handed me a Coke, and gestured toward the man. "Was this Mannes guy good to the Tucker family?"

"As nice as he was to anyone. He wasn't their choice. They wanted Captain Upton Bridges. They had talked to him several times over the year, but like I said, he and the boat they wanted were out."

Ryan sat the can on the table. "So this family planned a trip for over a year, rented a boat, and picked out a captain. When the time came for them to leave, neither the boat nor the sailor were available. How could that be?"

"Mr. Randle wanted that particular boat and Captain Bridges. Mr. Randle gets what he wants."

I had been listening as I looked around the place. "What's so special about Mr. Randle?"

"Adam Randle owns this place and everything in it and around it. His daughter was getting married in LaPaz and he wanted to attend. I didn't know he was coming or I would have had a boat and crew ready so as not to ruin the Tucker's vacation."

Ryan stood and looked out the window. "So the owner of this place has no regard for the customers."

"Adam Randle has no regard for anything or anyone. Have you never heard of him? He's pretty famous. Why is this all so important to you folks?"

"The oldest girl, Ivy, was found dead on our front porch in St. Louis."

"How can that be? Those people have been lost for over ten years. The authorities did everything but drag the Sea of California to find them. I think they would have done that if they could have found a way."

I took a drink of my soda. "We don't know, Mr. Saylor, that's why we're here. Tell me more about Adam Randle. Why is he famous?" I asked.

Saylor took off his ball cap and scratched his head. "Adam supposedly murdered his wife. They didn't have enough proof to convict him, but you won't find a person who doesn't think he is guilty. Since then he has been the suspect in three more killings. They can never find enough evidence to put him away."

Ryan turned and nodded to me. "Let's go back to

Captain Mannes. How did he play into this. Did he work here all the time?"

Saylor walked back to the soda machine, bought an orange crush and nearly downed it in one long swallow. "He showed up with a new wife about three weeks before the trip. She was a mousey girl with long hair. Looked like she would blow away in a heavy wind. I don't know if I liked her or not. She was around me less than a week before they left. Most of the time, Mannes was huddled with the Tuckers discussing provisions and currents. The girl stood back and watched everyone. They took her along as a cook. I don't know if she could cook or not."

Ryan pointed out the window. "Can you show us a boat like the one they rented?"

"Sure, follow me."

The boats were varied in size, most were on lifts. The larger ones bobbed in the water with the wake. He stopped in front of a schooner. "It was like this, only they wanted a wooden one. This one is Kevlar and aluminum. We had the Tucker boat here for over a year. It had everything they listed. It was a beautiful thing. Hand made by Donavan Macy, an old time boat builder. He died years ago. The entire vessel inside and out was cypress."

Ryan took a step closer. "Do you find it strange the ship was reserved for a year, you customized it for the Tuckers and at the last minute, Adam Randle took it?"

"Yes. When they disappeared in the other schooner, I racked my brain to make a connection, but I couldn't. They didn't complain, yet I got the idea they were not happy with Mannes. At one time they came to the office and asked if I thought they would be able to handle the ship on their own. I told them the truth. Our insurance would not allow a vessel that size out without a licensed captain." Saylor stepped on deck and led the way. "This vessel is sixty-four feet long and thirty-four feet wide. The Iguana Volez, was seventy-two feet by thirty-six feet."

Ryan began to walk aft. " What happened to the original vessel they rented?"

"Mr. Randle sold it to someone on the east coast. They didn't sail it after the trip to the wedding, said it was too dangerous. A special truck with four men came to take it. They had chase cars and lead cars."

"I know my geography but I'm not familiar with the entire coast line. Is it even possible to sail to the east coast?" I asked.

Saylor pointed to a map on a table in the main cabin. "You could make it as far as the Rocky Mountains. Once you make it to the Continental Divide, you have to take small tributaries, nothing bigger than a canoe could get through. Besides, it is a 6000 mile trip."

"Back to the trip," Ryan said.

Reganald Saylor was a talkative man."The Mrs. Doctor was born and raised in La Paz. She sailed with her uncle on several trips, but she said they never stayed out more than a few days. The other Dr. Tucker was a city boy. We laughed about it."

Ryan started down below deck. "Do you know how they were going to sleep? I mean who would sleep where?"

"Yes, the kids were in the sleeping quarters in the back. The adults were in the two mid-cabins under the helm."

I walked to the other end of the boat. "Is there anything else you can think of that was odd or different from other trips that left from here?"

"No. Not off-hand."

We went back to the office. Ryan walked over to a map of the Baja on the wall. "Do you know where they were last seen?"

Saylor joined him and put his finger on the map. "The last sighting of them was about here, at San Ignacio Lagoon. It's the biggest and best place to watch whales. Word has it, they stayed in the Lagoon area for three days. They went into the town of the same name about eight miles inland. Not much to do there except to tour the old mission or set up a whale watching tour." He shook his head. "They didn't need one of those. Once they left the Lagoon, they were never seen again. That was it. No word from them or about them until you came. The thought is they all perished at sea."

We talked as we walked back to the office and once more sat at the same table as before. I finished my soda and sat the can on the table. "So no bodies, no boat wreckage, no nothing?"

He pointed to an empty space on the wall. "I had the plank of wood with the name of the boat on it. It hung right there for almost a decade. One day it disappeared. Several other small pieces have surfaced over the years. Due to the currents they were found a great distance from the last sighting of the family."

Ryan took his phone from his back pocket and pulled up a picture of the plank we received when Ray was taken. "Is this the piece you had?"

He looked at the phone, up to Ryan's face, over to me, and back to the phone. "Where did you get that?"

Ryan answered. "It was left for us to find back in St. Louis."

The color drained from his face. "I guess the accident was no accident. I always thought Michael Mannes was a sleaze and maybe even a murderer, and one day he would show up somewhere in the world and we would know the truth. After five or six years passed I figured I was wrong. Now I have no idea the fate of the Tuckers. I do know it could not have been good. Some of the boat parts were scorched. Maybe it caught on fire."

I leaned forward and rested my elbows on the table top. "Our plan, Mr. Saylor, is to track down the truth. Ivy Tucker was only twenty-two. No one seems to know where she was all those years or how she got from San Ignacio to St. Louis or why someone killed her. I can think of only two reasons. One would be that she isn't the only one who survived the ordeal ten years ago, and of course there is the old tried and true, *follow the money*."

The man stood up. "I hope you find out the truth. If and when you do, will you tell me? I have wondered all these years. It would be nice to put it to rest."

I stood, as did Ryan. He looked at the older man. "We certainly will."

CHAPTER 10

Ryan called the pilot, who had serviced the plane, while we were at the boatyard. He told us the flight to Loreto would take over four hours. I looked at my phone for the time. The afternoon had slipped away and it was now six in the evening. Although it was late spring at home, the sun beat down on us like the middle of summer.

"I'll call Jackson back and tell him we'll leave after breakfast tomorrow. It'll give us a chance to make our plans, have a good dinner, and get a little rest. I need a shower. I forgot how hot it gets in the middle of the day. What do you think?"

I put my hand on his arm and leaned closer. "Sounds good. I'm tired and overwhelmed. I'd like to have some quiet time to think over what we learned today. The idea of a cool shower sounds wonderful. I feel like I could wring out this dress."

"It'll also give Jackson time to file a flight plan."

Once plans were made, we drove the rental car to the Posada Del Cortes Hotel and checked in. We didn't think our *friend* could have tracked us yet, but we were on guard.

The quaint inn had seven rooms which diminished the chances of *Mr. Who-Ever-He-Was* to stay there if he had managed to find us.

I went upstairs to our room while Ryan waited for a bellman to help with our luggage. He knocked when he arrived. I had to smile, our bellman turned out to be a young boy, maybe twelve. He supported a straw hat, white cotton trousers, a shirt made out of the same material, and had bare feet. Ryan gave him a big smile and a generous tip and sent him on his way. "Are you ready for dinner?"

"I don't think so. I'd like to but I haven't showered. Give me twenty minutes. Did you happen to catch a glimpse of the terrace? We could have a cold drink and relax before we head out into the heat again. The breeze is perfect and the entire space is in the shade."

"Sounds wonderful. I'll order something."

I heard him open the door to the balcony. I had a habit of going over every event of the day as if it were a movie. I remembered more of the conversation and my surroundings as I went over the scenes than I could at the time I experienced it. Colors brightened, people's mannerisms came up crisp and clear in my replays and inevitably, I came up with an important clue I missed before. I closed my eyes and let the movie run before me.

A shower renewed me. I washed my unruly hair and let tepid water run down my back until it turned cold. It wasn't until I got out to dry I realized I left my clothes on the bed.

Ryan came in off the deck and I heard him try to get us a room on the shore of the San Ignacio Lagoon. He hung up and turned to look at me. "Don't bother to get dressed on my account."

The blood ran from my toes to my head and my face turned firey hot. "I can't believe you can embarrass me after all our time together. Let me get dressed. I want to show you something."

"Can't you show me the way you are?"

"Not if we plan to have dinner tonight."

He waited seated in a chair on the other side of the bed while I searched for something to wear. I held up a red sundress to see how wrinkled it was, he shook his head *yes*. Lots of redheads stayed away from oranges and reds. I loved colors, the brighter the better.

Once it was over my head, he came to me and kissed me hard on the lips. He put a hand on each shoulder and pushed me back so he could see my face. "You're beautiful. What do you want to show me?"

I led him into the bathroom. "It's the biggest bathtub I've ever seen. I could swim in it."

"I saw it in the brochure downstairs. It's a soaking tub. We can try it when we get back if you like."

I took his hand and led him out of the bathroom. "Do you have a restaurant in mind for dinner?"

"I heard the Yoyoya is only a short walk. Want to eat there?"

"Sure." I looked at the tray by the door. "Do you

want to let the drinks wait until we get back?"

"No, you take a glass to the terrace and I'll run through the shower. I could use a lighter weight shirt and shorts."

The walk to the cantina took less than five minutes. A cool evening breeze tickled our faces as we strolled. We ate on the patio. Our meal included fish tacos, Dos Equis, and Sopapillas for dessert.

The difference in temperature once the sun began to set and the vivid colors of the sky were mesmerizing. After dinner, we took a walk around the square before we headed back to the hotel.

Ryan excused himself to take a business call from Nathan. I put on a gown and laid on the bed to think. I didn't remember anything else until morning.

I woke to the smell of coffee. "Hi, sleepy head. I have coffee here but I couldn't scare up anything to resemble a bagel. I brought you a Concha."

"Um, smells good."

"Are you up for a forced vacation?"

I sat up. "Why? What happened?"

"Actually, nothing. The only place I could find at the San Ignacio Lagoon that had a vacancy is Camp Pachio. They have a room available tomorrow but it involves sharing a bathroom with several other people. If we wait three days, we can get a small room with a king bed and our own bathroom."

"So your plan is to sightsee on the way, right."

"Right. The drive to the Lagoon is about one hundred and seventy-five miles. I thought we could drive to Mulege first. It's eighty-four miles. We can have lunch there and see the sights. Santa Rosalia is thirty-eight miles farther. We can make a reservation there and spend a couple of days. It's another forty-five miles to San Ignacio. We can stay there a night and then head for the Lagoon. What do you say? Up for the adventure?"

"Always."

He sat next to me on the bed and kissed me. One kiss led to another and we whiled away the morning and most of the hottest part of the day.

We arrived in Mulege in time for dinner. The hotel sat on the bank of the Rio de Santa River. Before we checked in we ate Chiles Rellenos at a local restaurant.

The view from our room took my breath away. The Mulege lighthouse sat high above the city. The shadow looked as if it had spilled down the hill in front of it. It was a forty-five-minute walk. In the dark, with our recent history, it didn't seem like the thing to do.

Ryan bought a bottle of Adobe Guadalupe. In Mexico, they call their wine, *The Drink of the Gods.* We enjoyed the view, relaxed, sipped our wine and went to bed early.

After years on the job as a homicide detective and all the callouts I answered to in the middle of the night, I slept lightly. A presence woke me in the wee hours of the morning. I sat up and hit my head on an object above me. The lamp on the bedside table had been moved. I jumped off the bed to turn on the light in the bathroom and tripped over Ryan's body. He didn't move when I kicked him on my way down. My panic level rose as I landed on his cold damp body.

The lights flashed on and off several times. The light had come from outside since we were on the second floor, the person had to be on or in a building. I tried to get up, but I had hit my knee on the edge of the bed when I fell. It had swelled twice its size in the minute. I hesitated and watched the light.

I took a deep breath and forced myself to scoot to the bathroom door. I used the frame as leverage to help myself stand. I reached for the light switch and flipped it on.

A broken wine bottle lay next to Ryan and I could see the dampness on his body came from the wine. He had been hit so hard the bottle had broken.

"Ryan, Ryan. Can you hear me?"

Nothing.

I dialed 0 on the house phone. A Spanish speaking woman answered. "Police! Police!" I screamed. I didn't hang up.

While I waited for help I rubbed Ryan's back and spoke softly to him. I turned my attention to the object over the bed. An oar. The kind you buy a child as a souvenir. In red, the words— *Want to take a boat ride?* were painted across its length.

Ryan began to stir and moan. His hair dripped with sweat, his skin was too grey. I tried to turn him over, but couldn't. Tears ran down my face. I tasted the salt in my mouth. We had underestimated our opponent once again.

An officer came into the room. "Did this man try to attack you?"

"No, no. Someone broke into our room and hit him. They also hung that oar over the bed. I patted

Ryan's back. "This is my fiancé Ryan Mead. I'm Kate Nash."

The policeman didn't take his eyes off mine. "Do you know anyone in this town?"

"No."

"Do you know why someone would do this?"

Yes, I did, but I didn't intend to tell him anything. Something told me to act as though the intrusion happened to be random.

I shrugged my shoulders. "Nothing I can put my finger on."

"Do you remember having a run-in with any of the locals on your trip?"

I knelt beside Ryan "No. Can you get him some help? I don't know how long he has been unconscious and bleeding."

"An ambulance is on the way. Things don't move here as quickly as they do in the US."

When I tried to stand for the third time, my leg didn't want to hold me up.

The officer, his name tag read, Captain Rodrigues, helped me sit on the bed. "You need to go to the hospital also."

Two men came into the room with a stretcher and put it next to Ryan. One of them bent over him, examined his head, turned him over, listened to his heart, and said something in Spanish to his partner. The other man handed something to the medic. He waved it under Ryan's nose and he stirred. When he did it a second time Ryan slapped it away.

He had his mouth near Ryan's ear. "Can you hear me?" Ryan tried to sit but fell back to the floor. "We need to take him to the hospital where we can rule out a skull fracture and observe him."

They didn't wait for permission. They loaded him on the cart and headed for the door. The captain walked over toward me. "Before you take him, have a look at his lady's knee."

"No, no. I can follow and have it looked at later. Just get him to the hospital. I'll be right behind you. I hated to cry. I couldn't hold it back. I started toward the door. My knee buckled but Rodrigues took my arm and helped me back to the bed. "What are you doing? I want to go now so I can find out if my fiancé is okay."

"I don't have a problem taking you there, but it would be best if you had more clothes on. My thought is that you would be embarrassed dressed as you are."

I had forgotten I'd gone to bed in one of Ryan's tees and some short shorts I brought for the beach. I slipped on jeans and my own shirt.

Other police officers came while I dressed. I heard him give them orders. I could only pick out a word here and there.

The captain drove me to the hospital in his police car. It looked like an ice cream truck with its red bubble twirling and blinking in the middle of the top. All it needed was music.

He let me sit in the front seat. "Do you want to tell me what is going on? I know it is more than you want to say. The message on the oar was personal."

I gave him all the pertinent information about both of us, but I gave him no details on the case we were trying to solve."

His next comment didn't surprise me. "I would

like for you to stay in town until we sort this mess out."

"I hope Ryan is okay and this doesn't take long. We have a reservation at Camp Pachio in two days."

"So you are here to whale watch?"

I looked out of the window and didn't answer. My main objective was to see Ryan. When we arrived at the hospital, he laid in a hallway on the same cart they had put him on in our room.

Officer Rodrigues guided me toward a row of folding chairs. "Wait here while I find out what they have learned about your fiancé's condition."

I didn't sit. I limped in behind him. When he stopped I pushed into the back of him. He turned my way and glared at me. "I asked you to wait."

I gave him my best flat-eyed stare. "I know."

Ryan looked my way and smiled. The bed held him at an upright angle from which he could see his surroundings. I walked over and took his hand. "I didn't protect us very well last night, did I?"

He took my hand in his. "Who was supposed to protect who? They want to do a C-scan on my head. If I don't have a fracture I can go."

I squeezed his hand. "I didn't wake up. Anything could have happened."

"The doctor said he thought whoever did this used chloroform. Not much defense against it. You were out, and I was fuzzy. I heard a sound. I thought maybe an aerosol can had fallen on the valve. The man hit me from behind."

"I guess our *friend* found us."

The officer overheard us. "Who is this *friend* you

speak of?"

We looked at one another. Ryan nodded yes to me. "A young lady's body, someone presumed dead for the last ten years, showed up on our doorstep."

He nodded. "And you believe the same man who hit Mr. Mead on the head and drugged both of you placed the body there?"

I sat on the edge of the hospital gurney. "Yes, we do."

"And do you know the name of the dead girl?"

"Ivy Tucker."

His previously dark face lost some of its color. "I know this case. Your FBI and Coast Guard, as well as the Mexican Police, investigated for months. They declared all persons on that ill-fated journey—lost at sea."

He had my interest. "Had you met any of the Tuckers or Michael Mannes and his wife?"

"I didn't have the pleasure of meeting the family, but I knew Mannes by reputation."

"Can you tell us about him?"

"Mr. Ryan, Miss Nash. I am supposed to be the one to ask the questions. Let's get this medical emergency handled, after, we will visit." He looked at me. "Let me get someone to look at your knee."

Ryan pulled me toward him. "This's getting more serious than ever. He doesn't have to follow us. He knows what happened, and the where and when. Our nameless man knew the boat came from Smith River, the family was last seen at the lagoon, and he knows what happened to them, maybe not Ivy until he murdered her. Think I should send Jackson back to pick up a few of the men?"

"The answer lies in how we have approached this. We have been all hush-hush and sneaky. We should bulldoze our way to the lagoon and let everyone along the way know why we are here. Let's make it difficult for him to get near us. We'll demand too much attention."

The officer came back into the room with a woman in a white coat. "I'm Doctor Martinez, an orthopedist. I'd like to look at your knee, perhaps get an X-Ray."

Thirty minutes later we knew Ryan had a concussion, and I had a hematoma under my knee cap. It was the cause of my pain. "Before I release you, I'd like to drain the fluid off your knee. You won't do any whale watching with the pressure. Trust me, the thought of the needle in your leg hurts much more than the actual procedure. Once we relieve the fluid, the pain will subside. I do suggest you ice it down in the evening."

An hour later we were back at the inn. There were no other rooms and the proprietor wasn't happy about the damage to the one we had been in. Ryan paid him for his trouble, the loss of the room, and a little more. He smiled at us when we left.

They reluctantly let us have one of the cabins near the beach. The captain assigned two men to watch over us. It was daylight by then, but we needed sleep and had nothing better to do.

I broke open one of the instant ice packs the hospital gave me and laid it on my knee. I had Ryan turn over and put the another cold pack on the back of his head. We were the walking wounded.

Officer Rodriguez said he would come back in

the evening to talk to us. He emphasized again the need for us to be there when he returned.

When we awoke several hours later we took hot showers, drank a glass of wine, and Ryan talked to Nathan. I laid on the bed but sleep evaded me.

Ryan laid next to me with his front side to my backside, which usually made me feel safe. This time it didn't help. Even though he remained still and didn't talk, I knew he wasn't asleep either by the sound of his breathing. I wanted to go over the events of the past two days in my mind. To do that, I needed quiet. His breath magnified in my ear. Instead of slow even breathing, he sounded like a chain saw.

I fell asleep somewhere in my process of reliving the earlier incident. When I awoke, the darkness of the room signaled the day had moved on. I turned over but Ryan no longer laid beside me. "Ryan. Ryan, where are you?"

A voice answered me. "Your boyfriend is fine. I gave him a sedative. You and I need to talk."

"Who are you?"

"You know who I am. I am the worst nightmare the Tuckers ever had. I don't want to be your worst nightmare, but if you don't go back where you belong, it could happen."

"Will you tell me what happened to the Tuckers?"

"They were whale watching. Three days after that, the boat caught on fire, everyone was either burned or drowned."

I so wanted to flip on a light. I had no idea where to find a switch, and I feared if I moved I would not live to tell my story. "How did Ivy survive?"

"I have no idea. I bet my life she was dead. I am only going to say this once. I know where you live, who your friends are, how much you love that cute little dog of yours, and every other detail I need to put an end to this and go back to my life. This is my last warning. Stop immediately."

I didn't hear another sound, and the heavy weight on my chest eased. For several minutes I sat still. My eyes had acclimated to the dark. No one was there but me.

Ryan walked in happy and healthy a little while later with a large bag of take out food. "Hi, you look pale, are you okay?" He put the food on the table and came toward me. Tears welled in my eyes and slid down my cheeks. "Did something happen?"

I didn't answer him. I ran to him, gave him the biggest hug and slapped him lightly on the chest. "How dare you leave without telling me. After all we have been through, didn't you think I would be worried?"

"Honey, when I left you were sound asleep. You didn't stir. One of the guards went with me to pick up dinner. The other stayed here to watch over you."

I stepped back and took a deep breath. "The killer came to see me. He told me he gave you a sedative and threatened to kill all of us if we didn't stop pursuing him. Are you sure the second guard is out there?"

"He is. I passed him on my way in. Your guy must have picked the lock on the sliding door. The policeman who went with me was stationed at that door. No one hurt me. I didn't see anyone out of the ordinary. Sit and let's have dinner while it's hot, and tell me all about it. What did he look like?"

I sat, opened one of the boxes but didn't take any food. "I didn't see him. His voice sounded like it came from the bathroom."

"What did he sound like? Did he have an accent?"

"I don't know. It was a male voice but it was distorted as if he talked through paper or maybe had tape over his mouth. He was hard to hear, but his meaning was crystal clear. He threatened me, you, Amy and Nathan and even Chili."

Ryan put both hands on the table and leaned toward me. "Did he mention the murders?"

"Yes, he said if they didn't die when the boat caught on fire, then they all drowned. When I told him Ivy lived, he said, *I'd bet my life on the fact she was dead. I will not let it be the end of me.*

Ryan leaned back in the chair, and ran his fingers through his hair. "I'm sorry. I'm sorry I left you alone. Do you think we should go home and let sleeping dogs lie?"

"No, but I take back my earlier idea about letting people know what we are doing here. Let's be your ordinary happy vacationers off on a great adventure to see the gray whales."

"Kate, what's your idea for after we find this man and have him arrested? Do you think you can prove any of it? Most of it is a theory."

"I have spent my last day without my weapon. I know they are on the plane. Can you have Jackson bring them to us?"

He stood and stretched. "You can't have a gun in Mexico. If you get caught, they'll say you're guilty and throw you in jail."

"Okay, then let's buy flare guns. I saw it in a movie. They can save your life if you're lost and will do great bodily harm to your enemy if you shoot him with it."

Ryan sat down and pushed the food my way. "That's positively gruesome. You should eat. You're not thinking straight. Our best course of action would be to go to the lagoon, join a whale watching tour, discreetly ask if any of the older captains remember the Tuckers, find out what we can, and move on."

Initially his comments angered me. I didn't want to back down. Then I realized it wasn't only me my decisions affected. "You're right. Could you call Nathan and tell them to be extra careful and to never leave the dogs alone?"

"Sure, do you want to speak to Amy?"

"Not right now, I need to think."

He kissed me on the forehead and went into the bedroom to make his call.

Captain Rodrigues came by early the next day and said there were no clues as to who assaulted us. No one saw the culprit, he left no fingerprints, and the workers and guests, where we stayed, had been accounted for. "You can continue with your whale watching trip. Be careful. Please stop on the way back and check in with me." He shook both of our hands and turned to leave. He stopped at the door and turned toward us. "The gun laws are strict in Mexico. If you are caught with one, the penalties are dire. I believe it's why your nemesis uses such strange methods to try to scare you. I trust you are as smart as he and will not bring guns into our country."

It was as though he had heard our conversation from the night before. Ryan took a step closer to him. "Captain, we intend to follow your rules. Our goal is to be more aware of our surroundings and the people around us. We will see you when we get back from our adventure at the lagoon."

"Vio con Dios," were his last words to us.

I turned to Ryan. "He told us *to go with God*, should we be more worried than we were before?"

He hugged me. "We had better get started. It is forty-one miles and I hear the last eight or nine are hazardous."

CHAPTER 11

We stowed our gear in the rented SUV. When we filled up with gas, the attendant was full of information. He handed Ryan an air gauge and a battery powered air pump. "Have you been to San Ignacio Lagoon before, Senor?"

"No."

"Okay. Bien. When you get off the paved road, you need to let five pounds of air out of each tire. The road is like a washboard. This will make the ride more tolerable and keep from ruining your tires. I doubt you will need the car once you get there. When you get back to the paved road, use this pump to air the tires up."

"Thanks for the help. See you in three days." We paid the bill and left.

The first leg of the trip to the lagoon was uneventful. We got to the unpaved road in about a half-an-hour. Then the fun began.

Ryan pulled over. "I guess this is where we let some air out of the tires."

From the looks of the road ahead of us, I didn't hold out much help it would do any good. It took over four hours to get to the camp, only eight miles away. We didn't talk on the way. I relished the time to go over the events of the past days. Ryan spent the time with a tight grip on the steering wheel. Every time our speed went over four miles an hour, the car bucked and bumped.

Our original reservation didn't appear to be valid. We missed our arrival day by twenty-four hours. The clerk relayed the news. "I'm sorry, sir. We are booked solid from December to June. This being the last week in May, everyone is trying to get in one more boat ride. I did take the liberty to call around and there is a cabin available at the Kuyima Eco-Lodge. The accommodations are a little primitive, but the food is superb, and they are famous for their friendly staff."

We thanked him and headed to the Eco-Lodge. They expected us and greeted us with friendly smiles, led us to our cabin and informed us the first whale watching tour we could take would be in ninety minutes.

The cabin was near the water, sat on stilts, and had a composting toilet attached. There were instructions in the bathroom as to how to take a bucket bath with the three gallons of water we were allowed to have daily for that purpose.

We locked everything in the car and proceeded to the shore where a panga awaited. It held eight people. As soon as everyone settled in their seat, we were on our way. "Ryan, have you whale watched before?"

"Yes, once off the coast of California. Nothing as exotic as this."

The panganero called for our attention. The boat went silent. "If you make a commotion, you will attract the friendlies. Most of them will be babies. They like to have their tongues rubbed. Please stay seated. If the animal is on one side, it will soon either move to the other or another whale will come up."

Everyone on the boat clapped their hands in the water or ran their arms from the water to the side of the boat.

A few minutes later, a baby gray whale surfaced. It was huge. "Ryan, won't a big one turn us over?"

"No, they are friendly and not aggressive. You can actually kiss one if you want."

"I'll pass."

Eleven whale graced us with their presence on our ninety-minute ride. We were told the next excursion would be at nine o'clock the next morning. I hung back to talk to the guide. "Have you heard or do you remember a time ten years ago when a family anchored off the lagoon and watched the whales for a few days. They were later lost at sea?"

He made a quick glance from me to Ryan and back to me. "That was a long time ago, Miss. Are you family?"

"No, I am an author and I'm writing a book on the tragedy. Can you add anything to my story?"

He looked around as if to see if anyone was close

enough to hear. "Manuel Ortiz took them in his pango for several days. I know he was sad to hear of their deaths. He has often spoken of the children over the years and how smart they were."

"Do you know where he is? Maybe I could interview him."

Ryan helped the man pull the boat out of the water and held it while the guide secured it so it would not break loose at high tide. "We transport the guests, eat supper with all of you in the palapa, and then we are free to visit. I will tell him what you are doing. If he is interested, he will find you." He smiled and walked off.

I took a little of my three gallons of water to wash my hands and face, brush my teeth, and wet my hair to try to get some of the tangles out of it from the windy boat ride. The effects of the salt water were palpable on my skin.

Ryan stood at the bathroom door. "I'll bring in the luggage."

By the time I finished, the bags were on the bed and Ryan stood and stared out the window to the Lagoon. "I had no idea it would be so gorgeous here. Let me wash up and we'll head for dinner."

I counted twelve cottages. Two were marked, *staff*. The rest were numbered, uno, dos, tres, and so on. We were in Ocho. The third cabin in the second row with a panoramic view of the entire camp.

We didn't have to worry about what to order. They didn't offer a menu. We sat at long tables with ten people on each side and were served by friendly men and women in street clothes. The meal was prepared with care. Chicken and spicy stewed tomatoes sprinkled with cheese and tortilla chips followed by chili lobster tacos, and Churros for dessert. We had a choice of beer, wine, or a margarita.

Ryan patted his belly. "If they feed us this way at every meal, I'll have to buy bigger clothes."

A man across the table laughed and introduced himself as Jerry Donnelson and his wife, Anna. "We have been here once before. If you take a walk on the beach a couple of times a day, it all evens out."

I offered the same courtesy. "I'm Kate, this is my husband, Ryan."

Ryan smiled and pushed his leg against mine. "I didn't see you on the pango. What cabin are you staying in?" He didn't pause long enough for either of us to answer. "There's a ride every couple of hours. You can go once a day included with your stay or pay extra to go a second time. If we get someone besides Captain Oztiz, we go a second time."

Ryan pointed toward the other people at the table. "Which one is he and what is so special about him?"

Jerry nodded at a man seated in the middle of the other side of the dinner table. "That's him. The man in the red shirt. They're all good, but there's something about him. I can't put my finger on it."

I kept the conversation going. "Can't you just get him for your first trip of the day?"

Anna had remained quiet until then. "It goes by cabin number. They want you to form a bond with your panganero. It's good business."

Everyone began to leave the table and find seats in a large common area. They were set in a circle around a fire. We joined them as did Jerry and Anna. I asked the couple, "So you've been here before?"

Anna looked down. "Several times. Once there was a family here from Chicago. They were traveling in a huge schooner anchored out to sea. The kids came in every day and went on tours with us. They always waited for Captain Ortiz. We decided to find out what was so special about him."

My heart pounded loudly in my chest. I wondered if anyone else could hear it. How odd of all the people who had been through the camp, they remembered and mentioned the Tuckers. "Have they been here since? I'm writing a book about a family from Chicago. They were lost at sea."

Jerry took a drink of his beer. "They're one in the same. It's an odd subject for a book isn't it?"

Anna put her hand on her husband's. "Oh, I don't think so. After they didn't show up at any of the ports they were scheduled to see along the way, I guess they questioned everyone who was here at the same time they were. That's how we know about it. The FBI came to our house."

I leaned toward Ryan. "We had better turn in if we want to be able to go site-seeing again tomorrow. It has been a long day."

Ryan agreed. We told them we looked forward to visiting again and went to our bungalow.

Once we were inside and safe I asked Ryan, "Don't you think it is strange the first and only people we met and bothered to talk to us knew

Captain Ortiz and knew about the Tuckers? With the incidents we have encountered so far, I think we need to be cautious."

"If I can get a signal, I'll call Jacob and have him run a background check on the Donnelsons."

"They didn't say where they were from."

"Neither did we. Jacob can start with their reservation here and work backward. Background checks have become his specialty." We laughed.

There were dozens of people in chairs by the water enjoying the evening. Instead of going to bed as we planned, we walked back outside to join them.

One of the captains talked to the group about the Lagoon. "It stretches sixteen miles into the desert and is five miles across at its widest point." An antelope stood on the other side to get a drink. "That is a Berrendo, known commonly as a pronghorn."

He had my attention. Ryan stood, took his phone from his pocket, and walked away from the group. I wanted to stay and hear more, yet our safety could have been in jeopardy, so I followed him.

"Jacob says the Donnelsons were indeed here the same time as the Tucker family. This Captain Ortiz is the one who took the children out to see the whales on several occasions. Since the case is so old, the records are open to the public, if one knows where to look."

A sudden wind came off the water and I stood closer to Ryan who put both arms around me and held me close. "I still don't want to get too friendly with them. We could get into a casual conversation with the wrong person."

Ryan kissed the back of my neck. "They could be the wrong people," I said.

He held me tighter. "I agree. Let's go back to the cabin. Whale watching begins early. I would like to take a walk on the beach tomorrow and try to speak to Captain Ortiz alone."

The next morning Jerry and Anna were at the table and saved us seats across from them. Anna leaned toward us as though she didn't want anyone to know. "There is a legend that a child washed up on shore a few weeks after the Tuckers left here. According to the story, the kid was so sunburned and dehydrated, it was unknown if it was a boy or a girl."

I didn't want to sound too excited about the information. "You didn't mention it last night."

Jerry took a drink of his orange juice and took a concha off a plate being passed around. "We hadn't thought about it much in years. Our conversation with you last night brought up some buried memories."

Ryan asked, "Does anyone know who found the body, or if the child lived or died?"

"No. It was all hush-hush. I do know it turned out to be a girl and someone hid her in the village. As the story goes, no one saw her outside of those who tended her. I've tried for years to find out more." Anna reached my way to get the butter. She saw the look I gave her and tried to explain. "We are just nosey. It's an unnerving story. The ship they were in was huge. The kids were a dream. None of us saw the rest of the family, but I don't think anything was wrong. They were too happy to be hiding anything."

I took a chance and pushed her a little in hopes I could get more information. "According to my notes and research, there were two more people on the boat along with the family. One was Michael Mannes, the captain, and the other was his wife. Did you hear anything about them?"

They looked at one another then Jerry said, "No. I had no idea there was anyone on the boat besides the Tuckers."

Anna scooted her chair away from the table. "A pango with Ortiz at the helm will leave in about ten minutes. We are on our way there now. You might want to come along."

We followed.

Miguel Ortiz looked to be a man in his fifties. His skin was that of one who had spent a lifetime in the sun. He smiled at each person as they stepped into the boat. His teeth shined vividly white against his dark skin. I finally knew what Anna meant when she described the man as ruggedly handsome.

Six people were on the boat, not including us or the Donnelsens. The wind blew from the North. I covered my head as best I could with the hood of my sweatshirt. Ryan wore a St. Louis Cardinal's baseball cap backward so the wind couldn't catch it.

A mother whale pushed her baby near the boat to show her off. She dived and rolled. The little whale opened its mouth and the captain lightly rubbed its tongue. They hung near the boat the entire ninety-minutes we were out. The immense size of the animals was a sight to behold. I wanted to spend the ride observing the panganero, yet the whales were so amazing, they commanded my entire attention until we were once again on dry land. Ryan and I hung back and stayed out of the way while Ortiz answered questions and chatted with the others as they stepped out of the pango.

When the last person left the area, he looked up to us and asked, "Is there something I am able to help you with?"

He spoke English with a thick Spanish accent I could have listened to all night.

I took a step toward him and looked around to make sure no one stood within hearing distance. "My name is Kate Nash. I am an author. I am researching and writing a book about the heartbreaking story of the Tucker family."

He glanced at Ryan and then back to me. "What could you say? The family drowned or burned up in the boat. No one seems to know what happened. Why is it important to you after all these years?"

I took a deep breath. "Ivy Tucker was found dead in the United States about a month ago. It changes the dynamic of the story. Someone had to know she was alive all those years."

He took his hat off and wiped his forehead. It had to have been a nervous gesture, the wind killed any heat of the day. "Do you think the authorities will reopen the case and return here to try to find out how she lived and who hid her?"

Ryan had stayed back but now stepped up. "Why do you think they would come here? What do you know? Is it true someone found a person afloat on the ocean and brought him ashore? Before you answer, I will tell you, the authorities are not going to do anything. The people were all declared dead three years ago. The estate is settled and the insurance money paid. To open the case now would be a house of cards. It would change everything. They don't want to do that. After all this time, their family home has been sold, their belongings disposed of and were it not for the stories in the U.S. papers, I believe they would be forgotten by most."

He held his hat in his hands and moved them around the band. "How did she die?"

Ryan told him. "She was murdered. Someone injected her with snake venom. The worse thing that could happen, if we track down the truth, is a killer could be brought to justice."

"Or get yourselves killed." He stopped talking and looked around. No one openly watched usT so he went on. "Go for a walk on the beach tonight. I will meet you in the break of the hills. You will see it when you come to it. Be careful. There are coyotes and they are aggressive. They won't hurt you if you are aware and speak harshly to them."

"Oh. We'll be careful. You can count on it."

CHAPTER 12

We explored the camp for the rest of the day. The scenery was all the entertainment we needed to keep our attention until the dinner horn blew. As usual Jerry and Anna were close. The seats they saved were between them. Jerry sat beside Ryan then Anna, and me on the end.

Dinner tasted outrageously delicious. There were warming dishes filled with handmade tortillas. Along the tables were large bowls of chopped chicken, pieces of tender beef, tomatoes, onion, avocado, and lettuce. If you were adventurous bowls of orange-avocado and red pepper sauce. For people like me who didn't want to test their stomach there was salsa, Pico de gallo, and sour cream.

Dessert, for those who were not too stuffed after the meal they served large slices of Mexican Dump

Cake with almond slivers and optional caramel sauce no one passed up.

It was twilight when we finished dinner. We casually walked to the beach toward the hills until we came to a deep separation with a high mound on each side. Miguel Ortiz stood in the shadows at the back where the two came together. Ryan and I looked several times in each direction before we stepped off the shoreline and into the darkness.

He began to talk as soon as we reached him. "Almost eleven years ago a schooner pulled up and anchored just outside the entrance to the lagoon. The mouth of the lagoon is much too narrow for anything bigger than a pango to navigate. Three kids came through the narrow straights and into the upper waters in a small vessel I thought was a lifeboat.

"One of the children was a young girl about ten or twelve. She was a beautiful child, bright red hair, freckles, and a perpetual smile. They stayed four days. I couldn't put my finger on it, but I had a bad feeling something was wrong.

"On the fourth day, the kids left, the whalers said they sailed off the next day. I never saw an adult anywhere, but then I didn't go outside the straights.

"I can't tell you exactly how long it was, but well over a week, before Samuel Garcia, one of the old-timers, came to me late one evening and wanted to show me something."

He stopped talking. I hoped he didn't intend to stop telling his story, instead, he sat down cross-legged on the sand. Ryan did the same. He picked up a stick and began to doodle on the soft sand in front of him. "What I am about to tell you could get many people in trouble, maybe so much trouble they could spend the rest of their lives in prison.

"I need your word, when you write this book, you pick a different town and different names."

I held my hand up as people do when they are sworn into court. "I promise. My intent is not to ruin anyone's life."

"Samual was old and worn out from years on the water. I followed him to his ship and he showed me a body. It was difficult to tell if it was a boy or a girl. But I knew it was Ivy. I could tell by her hair. She laid on a *play board*, the kind they have on ships and boats for you to relax in the water. It was blue and had a white mesh bottom.

"He didn't know what to do. We neither one of us, thought she would live. I waited until the middle of the night and met him at the water's edge and I took the girl."

I had been standing. I sat next to the men and completed a triangle. "What did you do with her?"

"I took her to an old nun who lived in the Convento de Mexico City for years. You can find her at this address." He handed me a piece of folded paper. "These people risked their lives and prison to protect the girl. You must keep the secret." The pain he felt when I told him she was dead showed on his face and the way his head hung toward his waist."

I took the paper and promised once again to keep the secret.

He turned and began to climb the hill behind him. "Mamasita Maria lives about a mile past the Mission. Don't drive your car to her house. Park it in front of the church, take the tour, have lunch, and leisurely take a walk. Go East, behind the church. Don't be followed."

A second later he disappeared into the dark landscape.

The night had turned black. The only light came from the fires at the camp. We followed the trail we had come down. We didn't talk. There was no way to tell if a person or persons spied on our meeting. Visibility to the front barely gave us enough light to see where we should step. The closer we came to the camp, the brighter the fire became. Behind me, I couldn't see anything past my outstretched arm.

The closer we got to the camp, the louder the voices. They came from people seated in the chairs around a campfire laughing and talking.

One of the hosts slid two chairs and the circle widened to let us in. I spied Jerry and Anna on the other side and waved to them. Jerry held up a beer he'd been drinking and tipped it toward us in a friendly gesture. Anna waved.

We sat around the fire with the others for nearly two hours. Ryan talked to the man on his right. By the time we reached our cabin it had been freshened. Three fresh clean buckets of water for each of us sat on the porch. My hopes about if I didn't use my three gallons of water for my bucket bath the night before, it would be waiting for me, plus the day's ration turned out to be a false assumption.

Ryan sat on the bed to check his email and texts. I came in from the bathroom. "Can you help me wash my hair? I can't waste any water. There won't be enough to bathe."

He stood and walked toward me. "This could be fun. What should I do?"

"Let's step outside. You wet it, I'll wash it, and you rinse it."

He went out first with the bucket in his hand. "Any place in particular?"

I walked around the side of the cottage away from the wind. "This is great."

Ryan poured the warm water over my scalp and hair. I worked through the curly mess with my fingertips to get it damp everywhere. "Do you think it is safe to talk here?"

"I do. What we're doing isn't conducive to conversation. I believe no one will be listening."

He poured another small amount of water on my hair and I put on the shampoo to lather the salt water and dirt out of it. I faced him and stood straight as I sudsed it. "I agree with everything Miguel said. Let's follow his instructions. I'm excited to meet the lady in question."

I bent over at the waist and he poured water over my soapy hair to rinse the shampoo out. "I think if the woman took care of Ivy for all of those years, she should know what happened. We'll have to gain her trust for her to tell us her story."

I wrapped my hair in a towel. "I don't know if it is clean. It feels better. I'm going to take the rest inside and finish a bath."

"How do you bathe in a gallon and a half of water, because that is all you have? I'd be more than happy to sell you a gallon of mine."

I stifled a laugh. "There is no doubt in my mind

the price I would have to pay would be more than I have the energy to deal with tonight. When I was twelve I went to wilderness camp. There was a guide for every four girls. Our bath water came from a freezing stream as it ran by the base camp. She would give us a bucket to fill in the icy water. We would warm it over the fire, and take it to a bath area cordoned off with large tarps. I haven't thought about this for years.

"We took a *Possible Bath.*"

He stood, bucket in one hand and one hand on the cabin as he leaned against it. "A *Possible Bath*?"

"Yes, you wash everything possible above your waist, everything possible below your waist, then you wash, *Possible.*"

He laughed and shook his head. "Go in and finish up. I'm going to check in with Nathan."

"Don't go too far," I said, "it may not be safe."

He kissed me. "I'll be fine. I'm going to sit in one of the chairs in the back. I'll only be a few minutes, then I need a *Possible Bath.*"

The day and the excitement of what might happen next wore me out. I laid on the bed and looked at my messages. The first was a picture of Amy holding Chili in one arm and Digger in the other. It made my day. I told myself I would not go to sleep until Ryan came in, but something about wind, water, and good food made it impossible.

CHAPTER 13

We ate breakfast before we left for San Ignacio. We decided it would stir up less attention if we ate breakfast and waited for the first excursion to leave before we went to town. The Donnelsons sat across the table from us. Jerry reached for the butter. "Are you waiting for Captain Ortiz today?"

Ryan pushed the butter in his direction. "No, we're going out with whoever is available. I want to experience it all. I noticed different panganero go to different places. Maybe we'll see a bigger whale today."

Anna looked at her husband. "Do you think we're missing out by going with Miguel all the time?"

He patted her hand. "We can try someone else tomorrow if you like?"

I stood. "It was nice seeing you two again." I

looked at Ryan. "We need to get the camera and sunscreen from our room."

"Yes, we do. We'll see you two tonight."

Ryan took my hand and off we went. We left the car parked under a tree the day we checked in. Ryan backed it out. Another bumpy, back-breaking ride. It took another four hours to get the eight miles to the paved road.

The Mission dated back to the late seventeen hundreds. Inside statues from a time long ago stood out against gorgeous stained glass windows. We took our time and explored the entire church before we walked out the back door and headed East. The old village held my interest with its one of a kind buildings and fragrant colorful flowers. The houses were stucco and painted in odd combinations of colors, a mustard yellow, salmon, teal blue and bits of white. It reminded me of pictures I'd seen of movie lots.

The old woman's house sat at the back edge of its lot. It was barely visible from the street with its clematis climbing to the roof and azaleas as tall as trees. We strolled up a small cobblestone path with grass poking between each crack in the ancient stone. The house looked alive. Climbing roses covered the entire front with a small clearing for the door.

The steps we climbed to reach the entrance held flower pots filled with blooming plants we had to move sideways to go from one step to the next. As I looked around to catch all the beauty, I spotted a small woman who sat on a porch swing to my left. Across from her were two chairs with a wicker table between them and a pitcher of liquid, too dark to be tea and too light to be beer, sitting on it along with three glasses. "Buenos Dias," she said.

It had never occurred to me she might not to speak English. "Buenos Dias. Yo, no hablo Espanol."

"It's okay. We shall speak Ingles." She had a faint accent." Please have a seat. Miguel told me about your visit and your purpose. I cried when I heard the news of Ivy Tucker's death. She was my constant companion for eight years. My eyes are dry now. No more tears will come."

I glanced at Ryan and then back to our hostess. "May I call you Maria?"

She nodded her head at me.

"We didn't have the pleasure of knowing Ivy. A month ago, I opened the front door of our house and a body, we later found out was Ivy, laid dead on the porch. She had this in her hand. Do you have any idea why she would have it?"

"No, I don't. Are you Kate Nash?"

"Yes."

She looked at Ryan with intense blue eyes. They were so out of place with her Mexican heritage and rugged wrinkled skin. "And who are you, Senor?"

"I'm Kate's soon to be husband."

She smiled and nodded her head. "The story of Ivy is a long and sad one and I'm not sure why I should or need to share it with you. What is your intent?"

Ryan leaned forward and spoke to her in the same soothing voice I heard him use when anyone got upset. "When we found Ivy, her age, fake identification, and Kate's business card in her pocket led us to believe we were to find her killer."

Maria turned her attention to me. "And your business is?"

"I'm a private investigator in St. Louis."

"And what do you investigate? You look hardly big enough to do work such as that."

Ryan reached over and put his hand on mine. I had a tendency to become angry if someone referred to my size or gender as if it disqualified me from doing my job. I took a second and paused to catch my breath. I told myself, *Peace. Be still.* There were several mantras I used. They allowed me to take a moment to calm down and not speak in anger. Ruth Bader Ginsberg said, *Reacting in anger or annoyance will not advance one's ability to persuade.* I had to admit, in some situations, none of those canticles worked. "Size is not a factor in my job. Before I became an investigator I analyzed and solved murders for the St. Louis Police."

"Do you have any ideas as to who this killer might be?"

"No, not yet. We have several clues. We know whoever is responsible doesn't want us to find out his identity. He has stopped us at every turn, yet we are determined."

"Would you like a glass of green sun tea? It's rather hot today."

We both indicated we did. She made no attempt to move so I stood and served the drinks along with napkins.

Maria leaned back in her seat, sipped on her tea, and looked off in the distance for a long minute before she began to speak. "Miguel told me you were an author and were writing a book about the sinking of the ship and the death of all aboard."

"I used it as a cover. People don't like to talk to investigators, and we know someone is following us. I thought it might make him back off a bit."

"And this has worked?"

"No, not really. Will you tell us about Ivy?"

"I shall. Almost eleven years ago, a whaler came to me. A child had washed up on shore next to his boat slip. The child had parched and cracked lips and clothes burnt to her skin. It was beyond the seaman's ability to help. He brought the half dead child to me. I peeled the material from her body, put aloe on her burns and gave her sips of water." She looked off again. She appeared to be in her eighties but with the climate and the sea mist hitting her all of her life, I couldn't be sure.

"Are you sure the story I tell you will stay with you and only be used to catch this killer?"

I refilled the glasses from the pitcher. When I handed her's back, I looked her in the eye and said, "I swear."

"It took weeks for her sunburn to heal, and years passed before she didn't run and hide if someone came to the house. She told me she had just turned twelve."

I interrupted her. "What happened to the fisherman?"

"Samuel Garcia. He died of a heart attack three years after he brought the girl here. I am sure he told no one what he had done. He remembered the pretty redheaded girl from the schooner the

Americans were in when the three children rowed the narrow straights to whale watch. Only the fishermen from the Sea saw the boat. It would not fit through the channel. None of the men on the big fishing boats saw anyone around the schooner, only the children.

"He didn't want to get involved. By the time she washed up on the rocks in the channel, everyone knew some sort of tragedy befell her family.

"All the information I could get from her was her name. She was terrified of someone or something. She hid in the cellar or the shed until our visitors would leave. One night, about three years into her life here, we had a storm. The lightning flashed and thunder rumbled. She ran into my room, got in bed next to me and began to cry." Maria stopped talking and stood. She couldn't have been over four-feet-five. She turned her head left to right and down. She had lost the ability to look up. "I'm an old woman. I must eat at the lunch hour or I won't have the strength to finish my story. Please join me. There is plenty."

She didn't wait for an answer. She opened the door and disappeared inside.

We followed. The house opened into the kitchen. A wooden table, well worn with time, was set for four people. The dishes were brightly colored pottery in reds and blues and yellows.

A young pretty senorita walked across a floor of hand-painted tiles to present us each with a fruit plate. She left and returned with a bowl of meatball soup and tortillas with shrimp, salsa, onions,avocado, and sliced peppers to dress them.

Ryan had been relatively quiet since our arrival. "Thanks for the lunch. You are a gracious hostess. We didn't expect the tea, much less this lavish lunch."

She looked toward the teen in the room. "This is my niece, Bonita. She spent many days and nights with Ivy over the years. She, like I, was devastated by the news of Ivy's death. Knowing the entire story, Bonita wanted to fix this nice lunch, and meet the people who will bring the killer of Ivy's family to justice." She looked up at the girl, " Sit dear and eat with us."

Once she said the *killer of the family*, my curiosity peeked until I could hardly eat. Had it not been so delicious, I might have sat silently until Maria began her story again.

Once lunch ended and the dishes were cleared, Bonita filled our glasses once again. We were asked to move to the living room.

I sat in a heavily brocaded blue chair across from a rocking chair our hostess chose. Ryan picked a sueded chair with a colored pattern in the same blue as my chair and bright red. Between us sat a table with conchos topped with either powdered sugar, cinnamon and sugar, or drizzled with honey.

Lunch filled me up and although the dessert looked amazing, we neither one touched it.

Maria took a fan from a magazine rack beside her and began to wave it slowly near her face. The room temperature was pleasant, She might have wanted to occupy her hands as she talked. "Ivy would not go to school. She didn't leave this compound even to walk into town. Bonita came after school and they talked. During the first few years, she was obsessed with any written word about her family and the tragedy. My neice bought every paper she could find and gave them to the child.

"Miguel Ortiz is my son-in-law. When his family traveled to bigger towns, he would bring back everything he could find about the Tuckers.

"We have saved Ivy's belongings since the day she arrived. In hopes one day she would come back to us. Bonita will bring them in for you to see."

It was as though it had been prearranged because immediately the girl stepped into the room with an arm full of literature. Ryan took it from her. He sat the stack on a table between Maria's chair and ours.

Conversation halted as we went over the articles. I asked Maria. "I see these are in Spanish with translations of some parts above the print. Can you explain it?"

"Si. Ivy was an extremely smart girl. Her mother was from LaPaz. She spoke Spanish as well as I do. She couldn't write it as well as she spoke and some words she didn't know. I wrote the English above the words."

"I see. Did she tell you what happened on the boat?" I asked.

Maria closed her eyes for a moment and when she opened them, a single tear rolled down her cheek. "What happened to that family would be too much for anyone to bear. For Ivy to live through it made her jumpy and afraid.

"The family left the lagoon and sailed toward the entrance to the Sea of Cortez.

"Ivy said she preferred to sleep on deck and watch the stars. The rest of the family, the captain and his wife slept in the cabins. About three days after they left the whales, she heard a commotion and blood curdling screams.

"She hid. He came out from below with a bloody knife in his hand. As he roamed the deck, she ran down the stairs to find her family. On her way down she saw a massive amount of blood.

"She ran up on deck and smelled smoke. The man put one of the lifeboats in the water. He saw her, ran, and grabbed her arm. He dragged her toward the boat. She said she knew he was going to kill her. But he looked over the side and his boat had drifted away. He turned to her and said, *not to worry little one. The boat will sink soon and this will all be over.* He jumped in, swam to the boat and left. The boat had a small electric motor.

"Ivy said she was determined to live to tell what happened to her family. The second lifeboat was not in its place. She found a toy float with a mesh bottom and threw it into the water, jumped in and paddled as far as she could away from the schooner. She thought she would sink when the boat went down because her float was so small and the boat so huge. When the wake hit her she held on for dear life. The next thing she remembered was waking up here."

Ryan wanted to ask some questions to clarify what he had heard. "Who was *He?*"

"She would never say. I always thought it must have been the captain otherwise she would have called him Dad, or Max."

"How could Samuel pick her out of the water from his boat slip when she would have floated the other way the entire time she spent in the water?"

"We never questioned him about it. He leased his boat from the Montego Fishing Company. He was not to take it out when he wasn't on a job for them. A lot of the men would go south into the deeper water to catch fish for themselves. I knew he did that so I let it go. He saved the girl and needed not to have been punished for it."

Ryan stood, stretched and walked to the back window. It seemed odd for the kitchen to be at the entrance and the living room to be in the back. The window looked out over a massive garden of fruit trees, bushes, and tropical plants of all kinds.

Maria rose and stood behind him. "Would you like to stroll in the gardens? This time of day the shade makes it pleasant even in the afternoon sun?"

We spent the next hour roaming around outside. I had only seen grounds as elaborate as hers in magazines. "Do you tend this by yourself?" I asked.

She pointed to a patch of multicolored flowers on the East side. "Ivy did all of the work on the section there. She worked hours. I would hear her cry and talk to herself as she planted and pulled weeds. We left her alone."

I moved closer to have a better look. "Why do you think she left after all of those years?"

Maria came to join me. "In the seventh year, several stories came out about the family. They called it an accident and told how the entire family plus the captain and his wife were declared dead.

"She didn't say anything for days. I mean

nothing. Out of the blue, she walked up to me and asked how she could get back to the States. She had no ID, no passport, nothing.

"I put the word out to some unsavory men who did illegal things. They came here a month or two later with the papers she needed to leave. I gave her money. I spend very little. She said her mother and father were rich doctors and as soon as she did what she had to do she would be back with my money."

Maria no longer held back her tears. I didn't know whether to go hug her or not. I decided against it.

We stood silently until Bonita came through the door with a box. She handed it to me.

I reached for it. "What is this?"

"I do not know. An unpleasant man brought it and said to give it to the American woman."

Ryan said nothing. He turned on his heel and walked around the side of the house toward the front.

He came back a few minutes later and shrugged his shoulders.

I looked at all of them. "Should I open it? I'm a bit nervous about the contents."

Ryan stepped up. "Would you rather I opened it?"

"No, it is addressed to me. Not exactly to me, *it reads Kate the detective who doesn't know when to stop.*"

There were steps to the porch garden entrance. I sat on the bottom one, put the box on my lap, and began to pull at the tape. I shook it. Nothing. "Oh my!"

Ryan sat beside me. "What is it?"

"It's pictures. They are of the inside of our house, my office, and inside the mansion. More pictures of Amy, Nathan, the dogs, and the men you left to guard them. There is a note. *This is my last warning. Stop now. Let this go. Ivy was dead all of those years. She is dead again and this mystery is over. Go home.*"

Ryan took his cell phone out of his back pocket. "I'll be back in a few. I am going to call the office and Nathan. I need to know how this could have happened."

Maria and Bonita went inside. I didn't move. I looked at the photos over and over again.

Ryan came closer to me. "The cameras were taken over remotely. Jacob said he caught it as soon as the alarm went off. He knows how they got into the system and swears it will never happen again. The burglar alarm went off at your office. The men responded but found a tech there who said he was from the monitoring service and he fixed it. Ronny tried to stop him, but he was too fast. He jumped in a cab and was gone. They lost him in Clayton traffic.

"Of course no one saw the man at the house. They handled it electronically. The person at the house could have been blocks away. The man at the office was small, dark-skinned, maybe Latino, and fast.

"Let's go. We need to get back to the camp. I don't want to navigate that horrible road at night."

I stood and put my hand on his chest. "I only want to see one more thing. It will only take a moment."

I asked our hostess if we could see Ivy's room.

Bonita led us to a small room near the kitchen. It, like the rest of the house, displayed bright, bold colors. On the walls were pen and ink drawings. They were good. The children in them were most likely Ivy's siblings. The pictures of her mother and father were so lifelike I recognized them. One man was depicted with a red devil mask above him and there was one in which her father stood holding his head in his hand. He had an odd smile on his face.

Maria let me capture them on my camera. She walked us to the door. "You two be careful. It took a monster to do the things Ivy described. If that demon is still alive, he could hurt you."

Ryan leaned over and gave her a peck on the cheek.

CHAPTER 14

Kate, he's out to scare us. Are you scared?"

"No, now that I know how he got the pictures, I feel better. Let's find him and get this over."

We were on the washboard road back to the camp. Our words sounded more like *noooot noooow. I feeeel betttter.*

I put my hand on Ryan's leg. "Maybe we should hold this conversation until we get out of the car. It is getting dark and we were told not to travel this route at night."

He took one hand off the steering wheel and put it on top of mine. "I'm hurrying. Top speed, if we don't want to tear up the car, is seven miles per hour."

"It's the longest eight miles I've ever traveled."

"Take this time to go over things in your mind. I'll get us back to camp before dark."

Ryan was right. I should use the time wisely. I did have several questions. Why didn't Ryan's men question the man in my office when the alarm sounded? How did he get in? The alarm company I used was Mead Security International. Ryan owned it and wouldn't give access to anyone but his own men. Was there more than one killer? The man we were looking for had to have help to get the pictures and still follow us to Mexico. At times I wondered how many people were after us, one at the house, one at my office, and one in Mexico. Maybe he wasn't where we were. Maybe he stayed in St. Louis and paid someone to deliver the pictures. Too many questions without answers. Ryan interrupted my thoughts. "You realize the Donnelsons will ask questions about where we've been."

"Let's tell them the truth. We toured the mission, had lunch at a quaint place, and strolled around the little town."

"See, I got you here safe and sound before dark." Immediately after he said the last word, shots rang out. We ducked down. The shells penetrated the back window and sailed right on through the front windshield. One second earlier and we would have been dead.

Excited voices came from every direction. Most of them shouted in Spanish. One man walked calmly to the car and asked us to step out. "I apologize Senor, Senorita. I don't know who did this, but we will find him. If he left by car, we can catch him on foot. If he ran into the woods, he won't get far. The people here have been here for years and know every inch of the area."

I shook from the ordeal. "What if he left by boat?"

"Not possible," he said. "We are in the upper waters of the lagoon. To maneuver the narrow channel cannot be done at night, not by the best sailor."

Ryan extended his arm to offer a handshake. "I'm Ryan Mead, this is Kate Nash."

"I know who you are and why you are here. I'm Agente Martin Hernandez of the Policia Federale."

Ryan and I glanced at one another. I spoke up. "Why are you here?"

People had gathered around. I'd venture to say everyone in the camp stood within fifty feet of us. The Donnelsons were mysteriously missing.

He turned to the people and said in extremely good English. "Sorry to alarm you all. A hunter was shooting. A mountain lion wandered too close to the camp and he went to take care of it."

There was an audible gasp from the crowd. "He got turned around and shot toward the road. The animal has since been trapped and is about to be relocated. You can all go on with your evening. Everyone is safe."

He gave his attention to us. "Follow me to the camp office. We will not be disturbed or overheard there."

It wasn't a friendly suggestion.

We went in and sat in the two seats in front of the desk where we were checked in two days earlier. The agent sat behind the desk and took a notebook from his shirt pocket, and read from it. "Ivy Tucker was found dead on your property. You traveled to Chicago, Illinois and spoke to the neighbor and people at the hospital where the Doctors Tucker practiced medicine. Since that time, many questions have come up about the Tucker case and to make a long story short, the authorities reopened the case."

I crossed my legs. "Why? What new information has come to light?"

"I'm not authorized to tell you much. I can tell you this is much bigger than a family being lost at sea. It includes facts the authorities want to stay hidden. The FBI and the Federale Police here are joining forces to find the truth. This is no job for amateurs. You should stop investigating now before one of you gets killed."

Two things I hated. One was being called short and incapable. The second was to be called an amateur. "I am NOT an amateur. I spent five years as a detective in the St. Louis Homicide Division. I'm a black belt in karate. I can take care of myself."

Ryan added, "As can I."

"I have my orders Senor and Seniorita. If need be I can drive you back to your plane myself and see you leave our country."

Ryan stood, indicating we were leaving. "We are on vacation, sir. We have one more day of whale watching here and then we are spending a week in LaPaz. There is certainly nothing wrong or illegal about our trip."

"No Mr. Meade, there is not. If you get in our way, you will find out what the inside of a Mexican jail looks like. It is not pleasant."

I stood next to Ryan. "Do you threaten all of your adversaries? I assure you. We want the same thing as you."

He stood, leaned over, put his hands on the desk palms down. "This is your last warning. Stay out of this."

We didn't go back to our cabin. Dinner time had snuck up on us. We found two seats around the campfire. The cooks prepared another mouthwatering meal. There were bottles of soft drinks, beer, and wine coolers stuck upside down in a massive tub of ice. Ryan got us each a drink.

I took a deep breath, resigned not to let something I couldn't fix at the moment, ruin a beautiful evening.

We whale watched with the Donnelsons the next day as though nothing happened.

On Sunday, we retraced the trip me made to San Ignacio Lagoon, in reverse. This time we drove the entire trip in one day and went straight to the airport. We didn't stop at the police department on our way back.

The Meade International airplane was in a hanger. We drove in and boarded.

Jackson, the pilot lounged in a seat with a beer and a pizza. He literally jumped when he saw Ryan. "Sorry Jackson. Didn't mean to scare you. Sit down, finish your dinner. Have you been sleeping on board?"

"Not exactly. I have a room at a nearby hotel. I came back the other night and someone was in the hanger. I chased him off. I have hung around since."

Ryan took the seat across from him. I sat on the

other side. "Did he do any damage?"

"No. I think I caught him on his way in. Just didn't want to get in the air and find out we had a problem."

"We were going to sleep here tonight, but we don't have to."

"By all means, sir, it is your plane."

I went to the bathroom at the back. "Jackson, you sleep in the single behind the cockpit and we'll sleep in the bedroom. That way we can be packed, keep an eye on the plane and be ready to go when they okay us."

The pilot took another bite of his dinner. "Are we still going to LaPaz?"

Ryan answered. "Yes. As soon as we can in the morning."

"Then the flight plan has been filed. It was what we discussed when you left. I just didn't expect you so soon."

I was exhausted, took a real shower and went to bed and left Ryan and Jackson to a hot game of Hearts.

CHAPTER 15

I dreamed of men with knifes, big guns, and somber faces, I dressed in black and hid from FBI agents searching for me and Ryan. I tossed and turned all night.

The flight to LaPaz took less than an hour, but making our way through customs took some time. I had an inkling the authorities wanted to see if we brought items pertinent to the case back from the Lagoon. By the time they were done, they knew what style and colors I preferred in underwear and whether Ryan liked boxers or briefs. I started to ask why we were in customs in the first place since we didn't leave the country. I knew I should leave well enough alone. Thankfully they didn't look at my phone and discover the pictures I took of Ivy's drawings.

Again, Jackson insisted he stay with the plane.

We checked into the Posada de as Flores La Paz.

Beautiful described it perfectly, it was a two story structure with a bright red tile roof. Beyond the front door, a swimming pool with crystal clear water, and small cabanas for those who wanted to stay in the shade. Barefoot waiters in tight black dress pants rolled up past their ankle and starched white shirts unbuttoned to the waist to show the deep sun tans and muscles scurried around with colorful drinks supporting umbrellas, and toothpicks in the shape of animals. They bowed deeply as they set the drinks and finger foods on each table, tucked their trays under their arm in a flashy dance move and backed out of the area.

The back of the building opened up to the Sea of Cortez. The sands were as white as snow and the sea different shades of blue and green depending on the depths.

Our suite was two story, the entire bottom floor had red, blue and yellow tile in a circular pattern that ended in front of the couch with a single green tile.

I knew the floor would be cool and damp from the constant traffic of vacationers going in and out to walk on the beach. The rear windows on both floors provided full views of the Sea of Cortez.

Although our goal was to find the childhood home of Sharon Tucker, we couldn't be in such a picturesque place and not explore. We put all of our belongings on the top floor. If someone broke in, they would have to take the time to go up a flight to look around. It might be a deterrent to nosey people.

The first day we snorkeled off Espiritu Santo Island. The place teamed with sea lions. They were huge. We kept our distance from them and they did the same.

The next day we ate dinner at a café near the hotel and took a bicycle ride to the El Comitan neighborhood where Sharon, then Gonzalez, lived as a child. Each street held a dozen or so stucco cookie cutter homes. Were it not for the different numbers on the gates and different taste in flowers, they were all alike. The residents were older. We saw no one younger than perhaps seventy. Some men in a park played Parcheesi, but stopped to answer our questions. A few remembered the pretty girl who visited her parents and became a doctor in America. Her parents moved away long ago.

The next morning we went to the library and looked up her high school and college yearbooks. Sharon excelled at every challenge she tackled, girls basketball, academic all-star in tennis. Quite the achiever.

The bike ride in the heat and sun wore us out. We spent a couple of hours under a cabana at the pool drinking Margaritas and eating cold peeled shrimp and oysters on a half shell.

Once rested we went to our room.

Ryan, who had been looking out the upstairs window turned toward me. "It gets more strange all the time. First, who takes their children out of school for an entire semester to take a sailing vacation? How do two prominent doctors from one of Chicago's biggest hospitals work it out so they can leave their practices for an extended length of time? And why is it the FBI, Federalies, and local police in at least a dozen municipalities can not find one clue in fourteen years? And lastly what are they so afraid we will discover?"

I walked over to stand beside him. "It seems as though they may have been running away. But away from what? Why plan so long and let everyone know your itinerary if you plan to disappear?"

"I wonder if the wrong captain was really a bad stroke of luck or if they did it on purpose. Maybe they are in hiding."

"Nothing we can do right this minute. Let's enjoy our last night here."

We sat on the balcony upstairs and looked out at the sea. "I miss my dog," I admitted.

Ryan filled my wine glass. "I'm ready to go home myself."

"I think we should give this a rest for a few weeks. Let's make the FBI, and every other interested party think we took the warning and are leaving it to the authorities. Then quietly look into the lives of the Tuckers more closely."

"I say yes to going home. Nathan doesn't like to be boss. He does a good job, but he only keeps things going. While I'm gone, nothing progresses."

* * * * *

I didn't think Chili would ever settle down when we arrived home. Digger acted nearly as bad. Ryan and I sat on opposite sides of the room. The dogs jumped from me to him and back again.

Amy walked behind me, leaned down and gave me a hug. "I am so glad you're back. I love your house but I'm ready to go home."

I patted the hand she had on my shoulder. "I bet you are. How did work go while I was gone?"

"We have a couple on the burner. Are you interested? Nathan is sweet, but let's face it, he's not good at the private investigation gig. He's an alarm man all the way."

Amy walked around and sat next to me. "One is a short change artist. It's more than one. Don's Malt Shop is run by teenagers. They do a good job, but someone shortchanges one of them at least once a week. I have it on the surveillance tapes. He goes in, orders a milkshake to go. He pays with a twenty or fifty dollar bill. The customer counts his change and then asked for change for the ten they gave him. He doesn't really give them the ten. It goes on like that. These kids aren't stupid. He's good. I think he could fool me."

"Do we need to take care of it tomorrow? I had visions of sleep, American food, and playing with Chili."

"Okay. We can begin Tuesday morning. It will give you a day."

Ryan and Nathan retreated to the patio. They looked as if they were in deep discussion so we didn't go out.

I stood and put Chili on the floor. She didn't want any part of that. She stood on her back legs and jumped over and over with a sad look in those dark eyes until I reached down and picked her up. "Let's have a glass of wine. Mexican wine is delicious, but I sure do miss good old California white."

Amy picked up Digger. It was like old times.

I was too tired to talk and Amy didn't seem to care. With Chili in my lap, I sipped my wine and stroked her fur. Digger snuggled with Amy. We sat in peaceful silence.

There's no place like home.

Nathan came in from the patio. "Are you ready to go home?" he asked Amy.

Amy stood, dog in hand and hugged him. "You bet."

I looked up from petting my dog. "Aren't you afraid?"

Nathan laughed. "No. While you were out of the country I put alarms on every window and door, along with lights that come on if something moves more than an inch. I also put them on the fence and the garage. I'd say we are safe." He reached in his pocket and took out a piece of paper. "This is the code to the alarms for your house. I did the same thing here. When the dogs go outside, the entire yard lights up like a baseball field. You might have complaints from the neighbors."

They took two suitcases with them and said they would pick up the rest in a day or two. With Digger under her arm and Nathan laden down with the bags, I whispered a little, *please keep us all safe*, as they walked out the door.

An hour later I finished my wine, took a hot shower and laid happily in my own bed.

Ryan checked on his other business. I didn't know when he came to bed. He didn't wake me.

On Thursday morning, Amy and I met at Starbucks on the Loop. It felt good to take a break and get back to my regular job. Amy had a latte and a bagel at the table for me. She pushed them in front of me when I sat down. "Hi. Our assignment is to find out who is short changing the teenage clerks at Don's or if the kids are skimming."

"I thought there was a video."

"No, I misunderstood. It was a YouTube video about how short changing is done."

I took a drink of my coffee. "How do you want to handle it?"

"We should have Ryan's guys install two new temporary cameras. One will catch the counter and the kid's hands and the other under the drive-through window will point to the drivers."

It had been a long time since we had an actual case together. I smiled. "Is there a walk up window?"

"There are two. One where the customer orders and pays and a second where they pick up the treats. Most of the sleight of hand takes place at the walk up window. The girl at the drive-through takes the money, turns to the cash register and then back to the customer. She puts the money in a little holder on the cash drawer where she and the customer can both see it. No one can say they gave her money they didn't."

I took the last sip of my latte. "This is a two cup morning. Want a refill?"

Amy picked up her fresh cup and blew on it. "I didn't talk to Nathan about the cameras. We were too busy. She offered her left hand for me to look at."

"Oh, my! You're engaged. That's terrific." I

stood and walked around the table to hug her. "Did you set a date?"

"Christmas. I don't have any family so we'll get married in Tyler at his childhood church with his family. Will you be my Maid of Honor? It will be a small wedding."

I held her at arm's length. "I would be honored. Has he picked a best man?"

"He wants to ask Ryan. You know how shy he is. It'll take him a few days to get around to it."

"You know Ryan will say *yes.*"

"I know. Back to the case. Will you call Ryan about the cameras? The store's open from ten a.m. to eleven p.m. so it'll have to be sometime outside of those hours."

I took out my phone and made the call. "I'll set it up." I talked to Ryan and put my hand over the phone to ask Amy who he should contact. " Lance Holt. He has been there full time since this started."

"I thought it was Don's."

"It was and it was doing so good, Lance didn't want to change it. He said he likes money over fame."

She cleared the table. "Are you ready to go? I think we'll have to learn some products and prices before Wednesday."

"That's only two days. Hope I can keep my mind off Ivy for a few days and focus on the job."

We spent five hours at the ice cream store where we took orders and money. It wasn't as difficult as I thought. Actually, I had fun. Lance turned out to be a twenty-something guy who bought a chain of four ice cream stores two years before, one of those high achievers. The store on St. Louis' Southside was the only place he had a problem with short-changers.

On the way home, Amy said, "I wish we could study short-changing before tomorrow. I've heard about it but never seen anybody do it, except for the one grainy film Lance gave me."

"I bet they have more than one video on YouTube. I'm convinced they have a film on everything. There's most likely one on how to do brain surgery or take out your own appendix," I said.

Amy took me back to her car and I followed her home. We looked up scams on the internet and watched until we found the exact one we wanted. After our fifteenth viewing we could have gone into business scamming people.

Nathan came in from work and when I hugged him he turned bright red. "I am so happy for the two of you. I've never seen two people more suited to one another."

Nathan hugged me back. "Except you and Ryan."

I smiled. "Speaking of Ryan, if I don't head home, he'll begin to worry."

Nathan gave Amy a quick kiss and walked me to my car. "Send us a text when you get home and inside so we don't worry."

"Will do."

Ryan's truck was in the garage. When I opened the door to the kitchen, delicious aromas attacked my nose. "What is that?"

"Beef Stroganoff."

"Really? It smells luscious."

He gave me a hello kiss and pulled a chair out for me to sit at the table. "It's simple. I thought since you worked all day I would treat you to a home-cooked meal."

"Whatever the reason. Thank you."

The table setting was elegant. He had thought of everything down to the tiniest detail. Salad bowls and forks, water glasses, plates for the stroganoff, and a dessert plate all were meticulously placed on a white lace tablecloth. "Should I be worried? Did I forget an occasion?"

He sat across from me and put his hand on the table. I put mine on top of his. "Mr. Meade, if you spoil me like this all the time, I'll get lazy."

"There is one thing. Did Amy tell you Nathan and she are getting married around Christmas?"

I looked at the engagement ring on my left hand. "Is that what this is all about?"

He looked down. "Maybe a little. We have dated for six years and lived together for four and a half of those. We don't fight. I love you and you love me. What's the holdup?"

I stood and went over to him. He rose to greet me. "Ryan. I love you. I don't want to change my name, for one thing."

"You can be Kate Nash as long as you want. Legally, your name would be Kathleen Madison Nash-Meade. My ego is strong enough to have a wife with a different name than mine."

I kissed him. "How about Thursday? I have a case on Wednesday. I know we can wrap that up in one day."

"We can have Nathan and Amy be our

witnesses."

"No. Just you and me and whoever's at the courthouse at the time."

"Why?"

"Because I am deliriously happy and I don't want to take a chance on too much changing in our life, superstitious, I guess."

We finished our dinner and spent the rest of the night practicing the finer points of married life.

I sat up in bed, wide awake in the wee hours of the morning. My dead husband Michael's essence and memory were vivid, I looked around to see if he was in the room. It had been nearly six years since he was murdered on a fishing trip with his brother.

Back then I worked as a homicide detective. Not one time did it cross my mind I wouldn't grow old with him.

Ryan had come to my rescue then and everytime I needed him over the years. We fell in love, yet in the back of my mind, I didn't think it was time to leave my dear husband.

I laid down, turned with the front of my body to Ryan's back and snuggled into him. Sleep didn't come. I left Chili tucked in bed, grabbed a throw and went to the patio. The stars twinkled in a clear sky. I turned Nathan's security lights off. A gentle breeze rustled the trees. I tucked my feet under me as I sat on the love seat. My mind skipped from one happy highpoint of my life with Michael to another.

I closed my eyes and imagined him next to me. A lite touch tickled my cheek, like a kiss, as though a feather brushed it. A warm breeze blew against my lips, yet nowhere else. When I opened my eyes,

Michael stood under a muted light at the back of the yard. He leaned on a tree. He wore the same clothes he had on the day I last saw him. His dark blond hair hung on his forehead and he brushed it away.

"Come to me," I whispered in my mind.

"I would love to but I can't, it's against the rules." He didn't move as he talked. The wind laid still. An apparition of my mind, I decided, yet so real. If I were a bit closer, I could touch him.

My gorgeous Michael, sweet, loving man. "Then why are you here?"

"To ease your mind." He stepped back farther into the shadow.

"Please, stay awhile."

"I've been here too long as it is. I came to tell you to move on. You have found another man who loves you. I release you with my blessing. Be happy, Kate." He waved, as he always did with two fingers to his lips followed by a kiss he sent my way. He disappeared.

I stared after him until I fell asleep. I was on the patio when Ryan found me in the morning. For the first time, I was at ease with my decision to marry Ryan.

Whether or not Michael appeared in the yard, he appeared in my mind. I put the incident back in my heart where it belonged. I couldn't bear the thought of sharing the memory with anyone.

CHAPTER 16

Amy and I opened the ice cream store at eleven. We hardly had time to count the change and turn on the machines before there were two cars in the drive-through and three customers at the walk-up window. Thank goodness Lance came in, followed by Cindy, one of the teenagers who worked there. I took orders. Lance and Abby made sundaes, malts, smoothies, and every other ice cream treat imaginable. In the middle of our busiest rush I whistled to Amy, who had manned the drive through.

A young man, no more than sixteen, came to my window and ordered an orange sherbet. He handed me a twenty dollar bill and grinned so big I could see his tonsils. He immediately asked, "Can I have change for this ten?" He shrewdly held back the ten.

"I need the ten dollars sir before I can change it."

He gave me a double-take. "I gave it to you."

"No, no you didn't." I persisted.

He fanned out his change to show me he did not have a ten dollar bill.

I apologized and changed the ten for him. While the exchange took place, Amy left her customers waiting and their treats unmade. She scampered out the back door, and came up behind him. He turned around, the big smile still on his face. I saw her guide him away from the window and out of ear shot of the other patrons before she motioned for me to join her.

A city police cruiser pulled up behind us. The boy visibly exhaled and looked smaller and not near as smiley as before. Amy went back inside to help Lance who had been swallowed up by ice cream lovers.

Without being asked he swore he only had the change for the twenty dollar bill I gave him minus his ice cream. I looked him straight in the eye. "Then how did you know what we wanted to talk to you about?"

He looked at me and then at the cop who now stood next to him.

The officer asked him to show the change. He reached in his front pocket and pulled out the correct amount. "Empty the rest of your pockets, son." The police officer insisted.

The additional money was stuffed into his back pocket. The cop put the kid in the back seat of the cruiser and leaned down to talk to him. "What's your name, young man?"

"Michael Moyer."

"How old are you Mike?"

"Sixteen."

The cop squatted and took a notebook and pen out of his front pocket. "According to the ladies inside, you have been stealing money from them for weeks. They say you have two friends who rip them off too. What are their names?"

"We didn't steal anything, we were only messing around. Do I have to tell you their names?"

The officer stood and told the boy to get out of the car. "I don't think you understand. Anytime you take something that's not yours, it's stealing.

"If you call taking money from a business every time you visit, *messing around,* you are traveling down the wrong road. If the owner here wants to press charges, you'll be in big trouble."

I wasn't sure how far the cop would go with his fear tactic.

He handed the notepad and pen to the boy and said again. "Write down their names. I know you think you're being a loyal friend by not telling. If the other two have the same outlook as you, they are going to end up in bad company."

He wrote two names on the paper and handed it back. The cop put him back into the car. "What's going to happen to them? " I asked.

"I'll take him to the station and put him in a holding cell by himself until his parents arrive. I need to talk to Lance and see if he wants to press charges. I don't believe he will. They'll all have to pay the money back, do some community service and hopefully learn the difference between messing around and committing a crime."

I had mixed feelings about the boy in the back

seat of the cruiser crying.

Amy and I collected our fee. The rest of the day we spent at our office in Clayton. There were emails to answer and dozens of phone messages. I worked for a half an hour before I kicked off my shoes and propped my feet on the desk. Amy sat in a chair on the other side and followed suit. She wore a pair of vivid orange cheaters low on her nose. She looked over them. "Okay, Kate, what's wrong? Are you still upset about the boys?"

"No. I can't get my mind off the Tucker family. I think about them constantly. I believe they were railroaded."

"By who?"

"Someone who knew the preparation they put into the planning of their trip and decided to ruin their plans and push them into their own agenda."

"I'm not sure I follow your train of thought."

"Do you and Nathan have plans for this evening?"

She took her feet off the desk and sat up straight. "No, just dinner and TV."

"Come over and join Ryan and me. I want to run my ideas by all of you. I'd rather not go through it twice."

"Sounds good. I'll call and run it by Nathan."

"I need to see what time Ryan will be home."

Twenty minutes later, we were on our way to Max's BBQ, in the city, to pick up sandwiches, cole slaw, potato salad, and buns. Nathan said he would swing by home and pick up Digger.

We all got to the house within five minutes of one another. Ryan and Nathan took the bags of food from Amy and me. Ryan stuck his nose next to a sack. "I haven't had BBQ in a long time. It smells marvelous."

Nathan opened the door. "Max's is where I learned how delicious it is to put cole slaw on a pulled pork sandwich."

We ate outside while Digger and Chili played tug-o-war with a toy squirrel. We were all having seconds as I began my story. "Since Ryan and I returned from Mexico, I have been putting together information on each person, actually starting in Chicago. The neighbor who gave us the information about the Tucker family and their ill- fated trip."

Ryan looked at me. "Such as."

"Let's get the Pictionary board out to make notes on. I think I can make a good case for why the entire family was killed."

They looked up from their plates with noteable frowns. "I meant after dinner."

Ryan went to a cabinet in the den, came back and set up the easel in the living room in front of the TV. He kept the magic marker. "I'm ready, give us your thoughts and I'll write them down."

"First, we went to the neighbor's house and she told us the Tuckers had planned the trip for two years or more. She said they had it right down to the minutest detail."

Ryan abbreviated my sentence and nodded at me to go on. "The woman at the travel agency said the trip was so well planned, all she could provide was a few maps."

Amy folded her legs and curled up with them under her. "The hospital where the doctors worked said they were obviously in love and they wanted to take a memorable trip. It dominated their conversation for the better part of six months."

"You'll have to enlighten us about what you heard on your trip. We haven't had time to talk about it," Nathan said.

I bent over, picked up both dogs and put them in my lap. "The boat rental is run by a Brit named Reginald Saylor. He told us the Tuckers had a boat and captain picked out before they arrived. The man who originally intended to sail for them was not in port. Saylor said the owner of the boat rental company wanted to use the schooner the family reserved so he could sail to Mexico for his daughter's wedding.

"They were forced to leave in another ship with a different captain and first mate. The boat they ended up with had been in dry-dock for a year and they completely redid it."

"I know where you're going with this, Kate," Ryan said. "Every person we spoke to said the children were polite, happy, and smart. For the three days they were docked in the waters just outside the lagoon, no one ever saw an adult. Not on deck, in the water for a swim, nowhere."

Nathan asked. "Don't you think if there was something wrong on the boat the kids would try to alert someone? It doesn't sound as if they were worried or upset."

I stopped to grab us all a cold beer. "It's the one thing that doesn't make sense. So, a few weeks later parts of a burnt schooner showed up about a day or two's sail from the lagoon. No one saw the boat go down or found any bodies. And nobody reported seeing any of the family after they left the whale watching lagoon. Where were they during that time?"

Ryan leaned forward to take a sip of beer. "You forgot one happening at the boat rental. A Latino man strolled into the building and when he saw us, he turned tail and headed away from there as fast as he could go. I know Saylor saw him because our eyes met when we both turned from the man back to the table. He didn't seem to think it was strange and we didn't bring it up."

I looked at Ryan, "I don't remember it. Maybe someone came to visit and when they realized the manager was busy, he moved on."

"Could be," Ryan said, "and I can only go on the feeling I had at the time. Something seemed off."

Amy folded her arms and hugged her shoulders. "This is giving me the willies. Maybe it was the man following us."

I looked at her. "Wait until you hear the rest of it. There was a couple who befriended us at the whale watching camp. I can't put my finger on what was wrong with them but they appeared to want to stay close, Jerry and Anna Donnelson. Later, while we were at the camp, we met a panganero who knew a whaler who found a child on a raft near where he docked his boat.

"An old lady who lived in the town nursed the child back to health. No one knew about the girl but the man who found her, the man who took her to the old lady, and the woman's niece. The girl was Ivy Tucker."

Amy adjusted her body. "Some story, what happened to the family?"

"The girl didn't say anything about the accident to the woman, Maria or her neice, Bonita, for seven years. The girl became stronger over the years and finally said the captain killed everyone on board with a knife, including his own wife. He took a lifeboat and was prepared to jump in it when he saw Ivy.

"His boat began to drift away. Before he left he told Ivy she would die anyway because he set the vessel on fire. Ivy found a child's float, climbed on. I already told you the rest.

"The more I think about the exact words Maria used, *Ivy ran down the stairs when she saw the man with the knife. She saw massive amounts of blood, and assumed her family had been slaughtered.*

"In other words, we don't know if they were dead or not. A twelve year old girl heard screams from below where her family slept. She saw a man with a knife and a lot of blood when she started below deck. Was the entire family dead or were they not?"

"What do you think it means?" Nathan asked.

"I believe there was something on board to make it worth the man's while to steal and run away. It could have been drugs, money, jewels, gold, or something equally valuable we haven't thought of.

"I'll bet when they remodeled the boat they built in places to store treasure. Whoever masterminded this tragedy forced the boat and the captain on the Tuckers. They were pawns.

"The Tuckers either found the stash or refused to

play along so he killed them. His name is Michael Mannes and he's the one who has been after us. He didn't have time to kill the girl that night on the ship and she was well taken care of and protected for years. Somehow he found out she had survived and didn't want her to tell her story to anyone. There is no statute of limitation on murder. It's my only guess as to what triggered him to go after Ivy." I couldn't hold back my tears. "An entire family slaughtered like animals for drugs or money."

Amy unfolded her legs and put her feet on the floor. "It makes sense, but we don't know the entire story and no one is around who could tell it to us. If the girl didn't go all the way down below, she didn't actually know if they were dead or not. A stab wound or two can bleed profusely."

Nathan said, "I vote for drugs. What else could it be considering the place and the circumstances?"

Our brains were mush, our bodies stiff, and the puppies begged for attention. We took a break and went outside with them. No one had much to say. We strolled around the yard and tossed balls to the dogs who would have eagerly brought them back a hundred times without tiring. We gravitated to the patio and sat.

Ryan spoke first. "I know we've read about the horrible deeds of the drug cartels but to know first hand it might have actually happened, it's unsettling to say the least. I'm not sure what we can do other than investigate each one of the people we think were involved and see they are made to pay for what they did."

"Do you think it will bring our stalker out again

to try to stop us?" Amy asked.

Nathan took her hand. "We'll be prepared this time. After we thoroughly investigate these people and find out their backgrounds we'll have the advantage of being able to identify them."

Ryan moved his chair closer to mine and put his arm on my shoulder. "I don't think we'll have to return to Mexico. Reginald Saylor's in California. Michael Mannes will come to the States as soon as he finds out we didn't stop our investigation. There's no reason to tell anyone about the old lady who took care of Ivy or the man who found her. He died several years ago. Mannes will be charged with Ivy's death, but no one will know what he did to her family unless he tells them."

I jumped up out of my chair. "Wait, I have proof. I have the drawings of the events on the boat. Ivy drew pictures of the man with the devil's face. Her drawings of whales and her ocean scenes are of art gallery quality. She was a talented child."

I passed my phone around. It didn't take long to realize I needed to have the pictures printed in a larger size. A lot of detail didn't show on a cell camera.

Amy broke the silence. "It's after eleven. My brain is fried and I need to get away from this. Let's not start our inquiry until tomorrow."

Ryan looked at me and smiled. "We have something important to do tomorrow. There's no rush now. Let's start on Friday."

"Friday it is." Nathan answered. They gathered their dog and belongings, we said our goodbyes and they headed home.

CHAPTER 17

Ryan and I sat in the living room, drank a glass of wine, and tried to relax. Neither of us wanted to attack the subject of Ivy Tucker. Ryan raised his glass and proposed a toast. "Here's to tomorrow."

"Oh, my. I don't want to say I forgot, because I didn't. I want to keep this private yet I feel horrible not telling Amy. Do you think it'll drive a wedge between her and me?"

"I would have told her and Nathan, but since I've been trying to get you to marry me for four years, I decided to do it your way."

I moved over next to him and laid my head on his shoulder. "That's why I love you. You allow me to make my own decisions, but that doesn't always mean I'm right."

He laughed and kissed me. "We had better get some sleep. Nine comes early when you go to bed late." He hugged me. "Is that the only reason you love me?"

"No, I love that you get up early and take Chili out for her morning run."

Chili heard her name and went to the patio door. We laughed and went outside with her.

Ryan was right, the morning came much sooner than I thought it should. The alarm went off and I pressed the snooze button.

"Come on sleepyhead," he said. "Other people are before and after us. We don't want to hold up the line."

I stretched and rolled over on top of him. He gently pushed me off. "That's such a good idea, but we don't have time."

It's not that I'd changed my mind. I wanted to get married yet I'd made no preparations. I hastily rifled through my closet and settled on a baby blue sundress, royal blue spike heels, pearl earrings and necklace and a cream colored summer blazer.

The closer we were to the court house the more my guilt blossomed. I didn't have a valid reason for my decision. I wasn't much of a friend after all we'd been through. I hoped Amy would forgive me.

Marriages took place on the second floor. We dropped by the week before to apply for our marriage license. I stopped outside the door and told myself this didn't and wouldn't change my relationship with Ryan. I loved him and our life as it was.

Ryan put his hand on the door plate to push it open and I laid my hand on top of his. I must have had a deer in the headlights look because he leaned down and kissed me gently on the forehead and whispered *I love you* into my ear.

We went inside where Nathan and Amy stood with smiles so big they distracted from every other facial feature.

I ran to Amy. "I'm so glad you're here."

She hugged me. "I wouldn't have missed it for the world."

I glanced up to Ryan who winked at me. He knew me so well.

Ryan handed Nathan my wedding ring and I reached into my jacket pocket and handed him a ring box. "You bought me a ring?" Ryan asked. He couldn't hide his surprise.

I reached up and kissed him on the cheek. "I love you."

The ceremony took less than ten minutes. The other couples in the room clapped and congratulated us.

We all four walked into the foyer and Ryan said, "Where would you like to eat, Mrs. Meade?"

"Is seafood okay with everyone." I hugged Amy again. "I'm so glad you're here."

"Why wouldn't I be? You're the sister I never had."

Dinner at Sosho Seafood was indescribably delicious. We said goodbye in the restaurant parking lot. The weather mirrored the day, beautiful. My new husband and I walked to the Arch and strolled around the grounds. Ryan took both of my hands in his. "I bought you a present for this auspicious occasion."

"You are my gift," I answered. "If I sat down

and put all of my thinking power toward targeting in on one item I want, but don't have, I couldn't do it. I honestly have everything I want."

"You might be a teeny bit upset when you get home."

"Ryan, what did you do?"

"You'll see when we get there."

Even though I couldn't think of anything I wanted or needed, I couldn't hide my excitement. The kid in me came out and I asked a million questions to try to guess what he bought.

I saw it when the garage door opened. My 1962 refurbished BMW had been moved over one spot and was replaced with a snow white Land Rover, Range Rover." I jumped out of the truck. "This is mine?"

He reached in his pocket and handed me a set of keys. "I know you love your car, but I know you are much more protected in this. The Beemer will last longer because you will no longer be four-wheeling in it."

I ran over and hugged him. "Want to go for a ride?"

"Sure."

We ran into the house, took Chili out to the bathroom, grabbed her lead and headed back to the garage. I had to use the running board to step up. I didn't care. The car had everything. I looked in the backseat. "What's that?"

Ryan had the vehicle fitted with a doggy harness and seat belt for Chili so she would be safe if we stopped quickly. "And what's that on the other side?"

He grinned showing his perfectly straight white teeth and the dimple in his chin. "I had a second doggy car guard put in just in case Digger wants to go for a ride too.

"Let's try it out."

I swear , Chili smiled.

Amy and Nathan said they would be at our house by eleven the next morning to help us study the life of the Tuckers more thoroughly. Our goal—find everyone involved in the killings and bring them to justice.

Mason's grocery store, in University City, delivered right to the door. We used their service several times before the Tucker case. When we opened the investigation once again, we would have to button up our outings and hunker down. I didn't want anyone to be hungry.

I heard a noise in one of the bedrooms. I held Chili in my arms and tiptoed toward the sound. There stood Jacob, the tech guy, two of his computer men, telephones, land lines, a private server, and five or six pieces of equipment I couldn't name. "What are you guys up to now?"

Ryan peeked over a stack of boxes. "I've watched you work. You like the bigger cases rather than catching a kid who learned to short-change. When Jacob is finished in here, we'll have a link to CODIS, the FBI database, a server, a tracing line, GPS tracking on the cars we drive, and the ability to put a tracker on any vehicle we want, and two of the newest computers available with all available software in your profession. It can do everything but tuck you in at night."

Chili wiggled to be put on the floor so she could greet Jacob. "Are some of the items you mentioned out of the perimeters of a private citizen?"

Jacob looked up. "Congratulations on your wedding, Mrs. Meade. Don't worry about the legality of the setup. I took care of it."

"Whoa, Jacob. I'm Kate and always will be. Professionally I'll be using my own name. But thanks for the good wishes. We are very happy. Now back to this computer network. Would it be in my best interest not to have any of the details?"

Jacob grinned at me. "It would be best, Kate."

Ryan stood twisting his wedding ring around and around on his finger. "Did I get the wrong size," I asked.

"No." He backed me out of the room until we had privacy. "This is something I've wanted for years. I waited a long time for the right woman. I didn't know you would buy me a wedding band. I've never worn a ring before. It might take me awhile to get used to it."

"Have you looked at the inside?'

"No, I haven't taken it off since you put it on me. I know you are going to make fun of me, but if I take it off, will you put it on me again?"

I kissed him. "You're so romantic. I've read stories about couples who won't take their rings off for fear of breaking the bond. You and I said a vow. I don't think we'll break it."

Ryan slipped the band from his finger and held it near his eyes. He read, *grow old with me, love, Kate.* It's perfect, as are you," he said in a whisper.

He handed me the ring, I slipped it on his finger

and raised his hand to my lips. The moment evaporated when Jacob called. "Hey, Ryan, got a minute?"

I dropped his hand. We reluctantly went our separate ways.

The food arrived a few hours later. Ryan came into the kitchen before I put any of it in the pantry. Boxes covered every counter and the table."Are you hungry?" he asked.

I laughed and opened my arms to encompass all the food. "No are you?"

He began to open the containers and separate their contents. He put like items together, noodles, spaghetti, and other dry goods in one pile, sauces in another, refrigerated foods in still another.

Amy and Nathan arrived before we had all the food put away. Amy surveyed the mountain of groceries. "What's all of this? Did you go shopping when you were hungry? That's a no no."

"I took Masons up on their order-on-line-and-we'll-deliver option. When everything in the store rolls by in print and all you have to do is check a little square, it's difficult not to overbuy."

Nathan began to toss items to Ryan who stood inside the pantry. They were having fun. I took time to greet Digger. Chili, at eight pounds, outweighed him. All of his hair made him look like the bigger of the two.

Ryan wanted to show our friends and partners the new room. They both let out audible gasps.

I hadn't seen it since they'd finished it. They had added a comfy couch with desk tops with the capability so swing over in front of it much like the tray tables in a hospital, only fancy.

Two fire engine red occasional chairs, large enough for a person to sleep in, had the same feature. There were two screens near the ceiling to view when someone occupied one of the chairs or the couch. On the wall behind the couch hung a huge screen I guessed to be at least six feet wide. The other two were four feet wide.

Nathan scanned the room. "Goodness, Ryan, what can we do with this?"

Ryan said, A better question, is what can't we do with it? No more calling Roger to use his equipment, no more waiting for an answer from the FBI. We can do it all right here. We also have a private server. I'd say we're ready to slay dragons."

Nathan sat in one of the chairs, Amy and I followed suit and sat on the royal blue couch. Amy had questions also. "What keeps someone from scrambling, eavesdropping, or hacking our server?"

"Jacob installed some sort of field around the room and everything goes through a satellite we own. I understand it seems like something out of the twenty-fifth century and I don't pretend to understand all the technology. I trust Jacob. He has been with me since his high school days. I sent him to Stanford to learn computer science. The dean said he could have taught the class.

"A friend of ours from Northwestern worked for MI-6. He let Jacob shadow him for two summers.

"The last thing is, I pay him what I think he's worth. Since he's irreplaceable to me, he makes enough to do what he wants when he wants. He's almost thirty now and happy as a lark."

I looked up to listen. I knew Jacob's loyalty to Ryan. "Let's see if this equipment works." I looked toward Ryan. "Can you run a background check on Reginald Saylor?"

"Sure, but first I want to show you something. Gather around." We surrounded his desk.

He took a small black notebook from a hidden drawer. "This is the manual. Since we are all new at this, the book is simple. And there is a list like this for every function. Go to B, Background check. 1-a, task complete. Feed information into 1b. copy and paste new information into machine 3. Wait for results. They will come out of the chute on 12. Got it? It's simple. The machines are numbered 1-14. The results will appear at the chute on 12. If it is going to pop up anywhere else the computer will let you know. It's as easy as A-B-C,1-2-3.

"Amy you go first. We'll get sodas and snacks so we aren't watching over your shoulder. Are you still a Pepsi girl?"

She sat at the desk and looked at everything. Tentatively, she opened the book and began the check. We left her to it.

Ten minutes later we returned with enough food to last through a Super Bowl Game. Amy sat with her feet on the desk and a smile on her face. "The most annoying part is waiting for the computer so you can go to the next step."

Ryan handed her a bottle of Pepsi. "Jacob said no request should take longer than twenty seconds."

She took her feet down and handed him a single sheet of paper.

Reginald LeRoy Saylor, born Sussex, England,

6/01/1955.

Served in Her Majesty's Royal Naval Service and achieved the rank of Commodore

Master's Degree in Oceanography and Coastal Science from Louisiana State University.

Employment: Coastal Labs, Miami Florida

Texas Petroleum Labs, Huston, Texas.

"He's an accomplished man. Impressive," Ryan said. "He could have been part of pushing the Tuckers into the second boat and using Michael Mannes as their captain, but I think not. When Mannes' name came up, he said straight forward, the man couldn't be trusted."

Nathan stood to stretch. "It's a puzzle. We could send someone to California to rent a boat to sail to the mainland of Mexico and see if they try to send a man with them. Maybe they hide contraband on every boat rented. Once we were at sea, we could search the boat."

"We can't go. With all our mishaps while we were in Mexico, everyone would know us."

Amy's voice broke when she spoke. "We can't go either. The man who attacked us knows who we are."

Ryan went to Amy and put his hand on her shoulder. "We don't need to go. We will be able to solve this mystery from the comfort of our home." He sounded confident.

I picked up the thread. "I think our best bet is to make the entire story public. Mention Saylor by name and say the rental company belongs to Randle. I try not to judge, yet what I have heard about him makes me cringe. As Ryan said, we won't have to go anywhere, they'll come after us."

"It's important to protect Maria," Ryan said.

"We can change her name in the story and say she died years ago. I'll use Ivy's drawings to prove the story is true."

Ryan leaned forward. "How can we prove she drew them and how do you know the pictures aren't the nightmares of a terrified child and nothing more?"

I looked at Amy and Nathan. "I'll have the pictures enlarged and printed tomorrow. We can all take a better look." I glanced toward Ryan. "I know you could be right. But the last pictures are of the boat on fire, a man jumping off, and the ship sinking. We know those are facts. It's the entire story, from beginning to end. We can use the pictures and put a caption on each one to tell the story.

"She went so far as to draw her rendition of the float she used to escape. The pango who rescued her and several more pictures of her family. The people are the same folks as in the photos and the news articles. No doubt she drew them. Each one is signed with IT in the corner written with a magic marker.

"It would make a wonderful book."

Amy crossed her legs and Digger moved to a more comfortable spot. "I love the little book idea, but we would have to send it to the people we think are involved. If it goes in a big circulation newspaper, it will be seen everywhere."

Ryan stood. "Okay, let's sleep on it. My head is spinning."

We all agreed and for the next few hours, we unwound on the patio drinking wine and talking about their wedding. The ceremony would take place in Tyler, Texas, the rose capital of the world. Nathan's parents rented the garden at the Rose Museum for the day. Amy was an only child whose mother died when she was twelve. Her father could not stand the pain of looking at Amy, who was the image of her mother and left. She'd never heard from him or saw him again. Nathan had three sisters, all older than he was. He looked embarrassed when Ryan pointed out he must have been spoiled."

We said goodnight. I hugged Amy and the guys shook hands. I knew we had decided not to mention the mystery anymore that night, but I had to tell them my idea. "Let's call the book, *The Untimely Death of Ivy Tucker.*"

Amy said she loved it, Nathan shook his head yes, and Ryan said, "Does that mind of yours ever stop thinking?"

Ryan said, "If it is your plan to do this book quickly, I'll have Jacob drop by. He has written and self-published two or three volumes of computer geek facts. They sell like hotcakes."

It took a minute for me to arrange my thoughts. "Do you think Jacob wants one more project?"

Nathan chuckled. "Anytime the man is asked to do a task that involves computers and computer work, he's like a kid in a candy store. He doesn't view it as work. He'd rather be in the computer lab at work than on a beach somewhere sunning himself."

Amy stood. "I guess we can't do anything else until Jacob works his magic. Nathan rented a small tiller. We're putting in a veggie garden this year. Any requests for a favorite summer goody? We are plotting it out on paper. So far, we have cantaloupe, watermelon, broccoli, cauliflower, peas, beans, cucumbers, and strawberries."

"Gees, that's a big garden," Ryan said.

I put Chili on the floor and went toward the kitchen where they'd drifted. "My childhood didn't lend itself to gardens. It was more sand and seashells. We did, however, visit the Farmer's Market and I learned to love kohlrabi and watermelon radishes."

Nathan took out the little notebook he carried in his back pocket and wrote down my choices. "How about you, Ryan?"

"Since you asked, I love butternut squash, zucchini, and spinach."

Amy leaned toward Nathan and looked at the list. "Looks like we've covered early spring, summer, and fall produce, I guess we had better get started. I want to order heirloom seeds from the Seed Saver's Exchange."

Ryan asked, "Do you have enough room for a garden that big?"

The two looked at one another and grinned, Amy talked while Nathan stood silent. "We bought the two lots behind my house. My place doesn't have near enough room for all his belongings. I never had wrenches and hammers and chain saws. And Digger has a bigger place to roam."

"Yes," Nathan added. "We have a contractor

coming to put in a privacy fence around the entire back and to put up a backyard shed for tools and storage. We don't want to move until we decide if we like the urban life. I know I do. Mom and Dad have several hundred acres and I loved it. Right now, we are close to work and you guys."

I never heard Nathan talk so much at one time. Ryan came and stood by me and put his arm around my shoulders. "We'd be happy to help since we plan to join in eating the spoils." He pulled me closer and laughed. "Wouldn't we, dear?"

I put my hand on his chest. "Yes dear, we would."

CHAPTER 18

Ryan and I took the owner of Bashan Motors and his wife to dinner. They owned the largest auto dealership in the bi-state area and carried seven upscale makes of cars. Leo Bashan and his wife Lynn lived three streets over. Ryan informed me Bashan wanted to be on a social basis with all the people with whom he did business.

His philosophy, according to my husband, was *people do not fire their friends.* He'd hired Ryan's company to update the security systems at all seven of his massive car lots, buildings, showrooms, and service facilities.

Leo thought thieves became bolder by the day and since he didn't sell a car less than fifty thousand dollars, keeping them safe and vandal free became a priority.

In my opinion, every person who worked for Leo

and Lynn were potential buyers and it behooved them to be friendly. Of course, I had always been a cynic.

We picked them up at their home in my new car, Ryan drove. I had no doubt it had come from Bashan Motors.

I learned a long time ago, when wealthy couples went out, one couple sat in the front and the other couple in the back. In my younger and poorer years, the gals sat in the back and the guys in the front. Rarely did the front seat chatter make it to the back and vise-versa.

Lynn had a stately figure. As she got in, she tucked her long willowy legs into the back with a practiced grace. Her salt and pepper hair feathered around her face in a stylish and expensive cut. Leo, who stood at least four inches shorter, had rugged good looks, silver hair, and the salesman's gift of gab.

My daddy had built me close to the ground. Petite, tiny, and itty-bitty were some of the names I had endured during my life. When I had my Glock with me, it evened out; Ryan refused to let me go to the dinner armed.

We pulled up to the front door of J. Gilbert's about thirty minutes later. Most of the conversation on the way over had been about their children and the activities they were involved in. Ryan and I were both quiet. Kids were something we didn't have and had only spoken of once. Personally, I hoped it didn't come up again. At the present time, Chili filled my needs in the nurturing department.

I liked Lynn. She was a gracious woman and a

humorous and knowledgeable dinner partner, as was Leo. The men had steak and although I had never considered myself a vegetarian, I rarely ate meat. Lynn and I shared an appetizer of Lobster nachos and our main course consisted of a salad and homemade bread.

Leo and Ryan chose Wagyu steaks, plank fries and a salad of micro greens.

As we prepared to leave the restaurant, a man bumped into me. He hit me so hard, I fell to my knees. Before Ryan and Leo could stop him, he bounded out the door and into a waiting taxi.

Both men helped me to my feet. My knee had sustained a raspberry almost as large as the ones I managed to acquire as a child when I ran too fast and my torso moved faster than my legs.

Ryan seethed. The owner came out as did the manager. "I don't know what to say Mr. Meade. I have never seen the man before. He ordered takeout which we discourage, and when he saw the four of you stand to leave, he turned without bothering to pick up his order and ran out."

"It isn't your fault Jeremy. Maybe he had an emergency. It doesn't matter now; the damage is done."

"At least let the house buy dinner for the four of you. It would make me feel better."

Ryan gave him a sincere grin. "It would make me feel worse."

Lynn had moved over to me and stood close. "I feel terrible. How rude people have become." She handed me a piece of paper. "This fell out of your jacket pocket as you stood."

I took the neatly folded paper and opened it. After I scanned it, I handed it to Ryan. He read it silently and shook his head. "How could he know that?"

Leo asked with a concerned tone. "Is everything all right?"

"Yes," Ryan answered. "We should probably go. We are stopping the flow of people in and out. I'm sure Kate would like to clean up."

The ride home was void of conversation. We drove up to their house by way of a long circular drive with lion's head pillars leading to the front door. Ryan got out with them. He placed a gentle kiss on Lynn's cheek and told her what a wonderful time we had. He and Leo shook hands. Both Bashan's stuck their heads down to look in the door and bid me a goodnight. "We must do this again." I heard Leo comment. "Of course, we can skip the part where your lovely wife gets knocked over. He placed his hand gently on the small of Lynn's back. They didn't turn around when the maid opened the door.

Ryan drove home, pulled into the garage, lowered the door, set the alarm, and turned toward me. "I have three burning questions. First, are you all right? Secondly, who was that man? And third, how in the hell did he find out about the book?"

I shrugged my shoulders. The house had been swept for bugs three times a day since we returned from Mexico. The book about Ivy and her family had been discussed only once, earlier in the day when Amy and Nathan were visiting.

We were stumped.

I opted for a long hot shower and antibiotic salve on my knee. I had a big pet reunion with Chili, who always acted as if I'd been gone for years, even if it had only been a minute.

I joined Ryan downstairs where he sat on the couch with a glass of wine, another sat on the table for me. A listening device sat next to my glass on the coffee table.

I sat next to him, picked my drink up with one hand and the device with the other. "Where was it?"

"On the coffee maker, it's magnetic. I believe someone stuck it in a grocery bag from Mason's before they were delivered. It attached itself to the first metal object it met."

"So, someone at the grocery store put it in?"

"Maybe not, anyone could have done it. Since everyone seems to know the four of us, I'll send one of the men to find out how the deliveries are handled. Nothing we can do tonight. Maybe, by morning, you'll decide to turn this over to the FBI." I didn't answer; I finished my wine and took the dog out to the patio.

I heard Ryan go upstairs. How well he knows me, I thought. He knew when I needed to be alone with my thoughts.

CHAPTER 19

Ryan sat on the bed, cell phone in hand. He wore a dark blue suit, a pin striped vest, crisp white shirt, and a red tie. "You look yummy," I said as I came out of bathroom. "Where are you headed?"

"The Red Bird Organization wants more security in the area the player's park their cars. Too many fans just happen to take the wrong exit and end up there."

"Do they really take the wrong exit?"

"No, but the other night a bunch of rowdies rooting for the other team hassled a couple of pitchers. Although nothing happened, they want a number pad on the door."

"And that requires a three-piece suit?"

He looked at me and asked. "Why all the questions?"

"I'm a little jumpy today. My heart tells me the

Tucker family deserves closure. The people who would do what they did to a family for no reason need to be stopped. We have no idea how many others have disappeared and been murdered by the same group."

Ryan came to me and took me in his arms. "Kate, are you sure they were killed for no reason? We didn't look very far into their past. We have focused on the trip and nothing else. Oh, yes, and we talked to the neighbor. Do we know she told us the truth? And the only thing that makes me sure they are dead is, if not, they would have been searching for Ivy.

"Whoever is behind this has made it abundantly clear we will pay a price if we continue. To me it sounds more personal than a killing over money or drugs. Now Ivy is dead, and the FBI is re-opening the case, why don't the killers let it go?" He pushed me gently away and held me at arm's length. "This place is a fortress. I doubt the White House has more gadgets and alarms than we do, yet they manage to know everything we do. Apparently, it is of supreme importance to them not to let this story and those drawings become public. I smell a rat."

"I know you are right. I believe everything you are saying."

"But…" he interrupted, "I doubt they had to kill the Tuckers. Some folks, usually those who live a total life of crime, don't care who they hurt. I've run into men who would kill for a pack of cigarettes. They're not going to let you take down a multibillion-dollar business if it is drugs. I say let's investigate the woman next door, dig deeper into the Tuckers life and if you still want to publish the pictures, I will help you."

"I know you're right. It has crossed my mind that the Tuckers might not be innocent victims. I don't know which would be worse, to find out they were innocent, or to find out they were not."

"I need Nathan back on the job. Have Amy help you. Look with fresh eyes. Widen your scope and see what pops up."

I sat on the edge of the bed with my feet on the floor and laid back so my head and upper body were flat. "We'll get started this morning. I think I will start where we began before, with the neighbor, Mrs. Caulfield."

He walked over, took my hands, and pulled me up to a sitting position. "Promise me one thing."

"What is it?"

"Take the morning off. Don't do anything about the Tucker family until this afternoon. When I get back, which will be in a few hours; we'll meet with Amy and Nathan and lay out our thoughts. Meanwhile I'd like you to stay home—read a book." He must have picked up my answer by the look on my face. "At least think about it. I won't be long."

He gave me another hug and a kiss I wouldn't soon forget, and then he was gone.

By the time Ryan returned, I'd cleaned the bathrooms, vacuumed the floors, done three loads of laundry, dusted the house, and taken a shower. The entire time I went over what Ryan said. Could the Tucker's have done something to bring on their horrendous fate? Nothing came to mind that three children and two doctors could do to enrage someone so violently as to drive them to kill, especially children.

I wanted to see Michael Mannes, and anyone else I could reach who had anything to do with the crime, rot in jail.

Two different reasons for Ryan's scrutiny of the case jumped out at me. The first, we were now married, and he wanted to keep close tabs on what I did. I dismissed it and went on to number two. Even when a case I had worked on that involved the mob, they didn't try to kill any of us, bug our cars, or follow us around. This had to be big.

Every day is full of infinite possibilities. Our scope is so narrow we can't comprehend anything outside of our own little corner of the world. Maybe there was another reason for what happened. I had never come across anyone in medicine. What could the two doctors have done? They didn't work in the same specialty. He was a pediatrician and she a surgeon, a brain surgeon.

Ryan came in through the garage. He had taken his jacket off and loosened his tie. With his pinstriped vest still buttoned, he looked more like a Las Vegas card dealer than a businessman. "What smells so good?"he asked as he turned the corner to enter the kitchen.

"I'm sautéing portabella mushrooms and asparagus tips in brown butter. I'm going to add them and mozzarella cheese to some omelets."

"What's the other smell?"

"Biscuits, dinner will be ready by the time you change clothes."

He kissed me first on the forehead and neck before he gave me a loving one on the lips. "Be right back," he said as he turned and headed for the stairs.

The conversation I wanted to have with Ryan would not go over well. I knew it wasn't a case of *I'm your husband and I said no.* In the years we had been together my husband, Michael, and three of our friends had been murdered. I had found a twin sister I didn't know I had, got kidnapped by a New Jersey crime family and saw to it my so-called mother and uncle were sentenced to live the rest of their respective lives in Federal custody.

He had every right to be worried. Like every other red-blooded person on the planet who didn't have some horrible illness, I thought myself invincible.

Ryan bounded down the stairs with Chili dog right behind him barking at his heels. I looked up. He had Chili's favorite toy just high enough above her she couldn't reach it. She showed him her displeasure by barking loudly. He stopped on the bottom step, gave the dog her toy and played tug-o-war with her for a few minutes. She sounded ferocious.

"You two are going to have to resume playtime later, dinner's ready." I fixed his plate and poured him a glass of Rosé.

"This looks wonderful and smells even better."

"After I had all those groceries delivered, I decided I should cook. I looked this dish up on Pinterest."

He raised his glass. "To Pinterest."

I toasted with him.

"Are we going to call the FBI today about the Tucker case and Ivy's drawings?"

I looked at him over my fork and said nothing.

"You aren't, are you?"

"No. I want to sleep on it. Don't you think if I call them and tell them we are going to widen our investigation, they might think I believe myself to be a better detective than they are? Didn't I hear the agent in Chicago say they would not reopen the case?"

"Then don't tell them, but remember, the officer in Mexico said they did reopen it. We can find out everything we need to know without leaving the house. Give it two weeks and then if we haven't found any new clues we will go on with the book. Those people have been around for the last fifteen years and haven't gone anywhere; I doubt they will in the next two weeks."

"I know you are right. Amy and I will talk to everyone again, ask different questions and add people to our list if need be. The pictures are so amazing. I'd love for the public to find out, through Ivy's eyes, what really happened."

He finished the food on his plate. "Do we have jelly? I haven't had biscuits and jelly since I was a small child."

I headed for the pantry. "Blueberry, blackberry, or grape?"

He was up before me headed toward the pantry. "Blackberry is my favorite." He said nothing else until he lathered half of the baked treat with jam.

We cleaned the dinner dishes as we drank the

rest of the wine. My mind was on making a list of things to ask the Chicago neighbor, then I remembered. "Want to head over to Amy's and Nathan's and look at the new land and garden? They are expecting us."

"Sounds good, I'd like to see what they've done." He picked up Chili and asked her, "Want to visit Digger tonight?" She barked. Ryan tucked her under his arm and said, "Okay, let's go."

On the way over we stopped at Ted Drew's and picked up a carton of black walnut frozen yogurt.

We went through the gate into the backyard and found Nathan and Amy. I sat Chili on the ground, Digger met her halfway. They met to chase one another around the huge space.

"We come bearing gifts." Ryan held out the ice cream.

Nathan looked up. "Hi guys. We could use a break." He put his hoe down. Amy, who had been kneeling on a garden pad, stood and stretched.

We all went inside. Amy and Nathan dished out the black walnut yogurt. We carried our desserts outside to the patio.

Amy handed me a spoon. "What have you decided to do about the book?"

I answered readily. "It is one reason we came over. The other being to see all the improvements you two have made."

Nathan spoke up. "Let's talk about the book first."

I looked at Ryan before I said anything. He shrugged his shoulders. "We had a long discussion about it. We decided there might be another reason why these men wanted to kill the Tuckers and it would be better to put the book on hold and investigate a little more."

I took over. "Yes, we assumed the Tuckers were in the wrong place at the wrong time. It might not be the case. Maybe they were on the run from something they couldn't fix. They made some permanent decisions before they left on their trip."

Amy held her spoon full of ice cream suspended near her mouth and said, "After what happened at the restaurant, Nathan and I came to the same conclusion. At this point what possible difference could it make if the story comes out. We checked and unless the people involved are dead, we can't use their real names. They would have to give written permission and we know that isn't going to happen."

I played with my ice cream, swirling it in the bowl. "I hadn't thought of that. Amy, let's me and you take a closer look at Mrs. Caulfield, the staff at the hospital, and what else went on in the Chicago area when the Tuckers decided to take a three-month cruise."

"I like it. We can start in the morning and use our new equipment to run background checks."

I took a bite. "What is the low-pitched hum I hear?"

Nathan grinned. "It's a device that keeps people from listening to our conversations. All they hear within a fifty-foot radius is a low annoying hum."

"Ryan," I said, "we need one of those."

He reached in his pocket and came out with two small boxes. He opened one and handed the other one to me. "Carry it in your pocket. You don't need to remove it for it to work. Reach in, push this button and talk away. We all four have one. The only thing we need to do now is remember to use them."

Nathan sat his bowl on the patio table between them. "You know we love and respect you two, but they did more than intimidate Amy. They could have killed her. We talked about it and we think she and I should sit this one out."

Kate reached over and touched Amy's arm. "I don't blame you. No hard feelings. We have cases stacking up at the agency. Maybe you could focus on those."

Amy looked at Nathan. "It's a good idea, but I can't work by myself."

Ryan looked at Nathan. "Do you want to work with her?"

"I'd love to," Nathan answered, "but we can't live on what the agency pays, and you said you needed me at the office." He stopped and looked toward Amy; she shook her head yes. "We're pregnant," he added.

I scurried to her chair and knelt beside her. "How wonderful!"

"We think so," Amy said, the joy evident in her voice. "The baby's due in January."

Ryan stood and offered his hand to Nathan, changed his mind and walked around the table to give his friend a hug. "I'm happy for you Nate. And so far as the money goes, you will draw your regular salary until this Tucker case is over. Then you can come back to your regular job and Kate can go back to hers." Ryan tried to act unconcerned, but he couldn't hide his uneasiness. "This shouldn't take over a week or two, unless they kill us right off the bat. Then it will only be a few days."

We looked at one another and the chatter stopped. We all knew how true his words could be.

CHAPTER 20

Ryan called the next day from his office. I could tell whatever his reason for the call, it wasn't good. "What happened?" I asked.

"I received a graphic text today. It describes in detail what they intend to do to you if you don't stop."

"Oh no, Ryan, who sent it?"

"Jacob can't track it. He has done everything. I called Roger. He is coming to get my phone later this evening."

"Someone is at the door."

"Kate. Don't take any chances. I know it's important to you to get Ivy's pictures off your phone and on to paper, but be careful. Two of my men are on the way over. They have a password. Its *Red feathers don't bend*. If they don't know it, shoot them and call the police."

"How do you come up with those?"

"I pick the most random words I can. Stay safe, I'm almost done here and should be home by six."

"Be careful. Do you have a bodyguard?"

"Yes, two actually."

I walked to the door and looked out the side window. I recognized both men, but I did as Ryan asked. They knew the password and I let them in.

"Hi Jeff, hi Matt, sorry to have to bring you over here."

"Not a problem, Mrs. Meade, it's what we do. What can we help you with?"

I picked up the manila envelopes I had to put my work in. "I need to take my phone to the office store. There are some cell phone pictures I'd like to have made into prints. I'd like to wait for them and bring them back with me," I added, "safely, and please, call me Kate."

"Are you ready to go, Mrs. a-a-Kate?" Jeff asked.

"Ready as I'll ever be."

No matter how many times I had bodyguards in my life, I never became comfortable with the concept. Both men were tall and lean, each had an ear bud I assumed kept him in contact with the other, or perhaps a third man out of sight somewhere.

Matt walked one step in front of me. His eyes and head never stopped moving. Jeff walked a half step behind me and to my left. Both men wore well-fitting suits with bulges where their side arms rested in shoulder holsters. I had my Glock and resisted the urge to pat it to reassure myself.

We stepped up to the SUV. It was new, shiny,

with bullet proof windows and dark tint. After the ordeal we had in New Jersey with my sister, Ryan put extra armor on all his company cars. This one had Meade Surveillance and Security in small gold letters on the driver's side door.

Matt put me in the car. Jeff walked around the back of the vehicle before entering on the passenger side.

When we arrived at the store, we did everything in reverse. Inside we walked to the printer counter in the back. The men stood one on each side until we were finished. Their eyes continually scanned the store for danger.

It could have been my imagination, but it seemed the man worked quickly on my order and asked several times if I was happy with his work. His hands shook as he handed me my package.

Before the men left me, they checked every room in the house, the garage, basement, and back yard.

I went into the nifty office Ryan and his techs set up and laid my work out on the table and desk. I began to work on the text.

I knew the book I worked on may never see the light of day, but I intended to finish it no matter what.

It was important I didn't accuse anyone of a crime. I needed to lay the story out, describe it with the aid of the drawings and let others draw their own conclusions. I would only give names to Ivy, her mom and dad, and her siblings.

The others I would identify as panganero, cook, captain, boat rental manager, and whale guide.

I knew if I did it correctly, it would help bring

the murderers to justice, or at least bring the possibility of foul play to the forefront.

Ryan came in as I worked. "Did the men take good care of you today?"

"Yes, I felt like a dignitary or royalty. Thanks. So, who do you think wants to kill me?"

"Anyone and everyone whose business will be interrupted or destroyed by this book, knowing you are not going to stop. I say we get it done as soon as possible and get it out in the open. Once it is all public, it won't matter. If they kill us then, it would be for revenge. Some of these people would murder their own mother for five dollars."

I panned the house with my hand. "How many bodyguards are out there?"

"Several," he said nonchalantly.

"How many?" I asked again.

"Six here and four outside Amy's— just in case."

I stood and walked away from my work. "Are you hungry? We could order a pizza."

He pulled me to him. "No, I don't want to take a chance of any more foreign objects making their way into the house. I'll make something. Neither of us needs the stress. I want this over with. Nathan is so excited about the baby he came to my office to talk to me. His opinion is it doesn't matter what he and Amy do. So long as this case is active, they are in danger. The bad guys have no idea they aren't working with us, even if they are off doing something else."

"I understand that," I said. "Maybe he will let Amy come help me with the grunt work and we can wrap it up. I'm okay with putting the work in the safe until later."

"Nathan should be okay with that arrangement so long as we have bodyguards. Let's find something to eat." He pushed me away so he could look into my eyes. "We guys have macho poured into our DNA. I don't mean to try to control you. Whatever we decide to do, let's do it quickly. When projects take too long, the other side tends to get antsy and they might do something else stupid.

"Whoever killed Ivy might think, what's one more? Where's Chili? She didn't come to greet me?"

I pulled away. "My goodness, I don't know. I took her with me to the store and I remember bringing her back into the house, I haven't seen her since."

"How long ago was that?"

"A couple of hours, I thought she found a good place to take a nap."

Ryan's phone buzzed at the same instant someone knocked on the door. "It's Matt. He has Chili. He saw a man put her down at the end of the block. She came running toward him."

I ran to the front door and threw it open. Chili had cuddled up against Matt, but she shook all over. I grabbed her. "Is she okay? She's not hurt, is she?"

"No." Matt answered and handed a piece of paper to Ryan. "This was attached to her collar. *See how easy this is?*

Ryan turned the note toward me so I could read it. I hugged Chili tighter. He turned to Matt. "How do you think he got her? This place is tighter than

Fort Knox."

Matt talked into a walkie-talkie on his sleeve. "Butch, take a light and go around the fence. Focus on the bottom. We need to find out how the dog got out."

Matt said, "I'll check the inside."

Ryan followed him. "I'll help."

A half-an-hour later, they came back inside. Matt talked. "Looks like someone dug a hole under the fence behind the forsythia bush and filled it with fresh meat. Chili must have gone after it and he grabbed her."

Ryan looked up at me. "How did she get outside in the first place?"

I was ashamed. "I opened the door a crack so she could come and go as she wanted so I could work on the book. I feel horrible."

Neither man said a word. It was obvious no one could make me feel worse than I already did.

I went to the office, turned off the lights and closed the door. For the rest of the night, I held Chili close to me, sat next to Ryan, and contemplated my actions.

I realized the death of the girl always occupied my mind. It would stay there until the people responsible paid for what they did. Even though I knew putting a few people in jail wouldn't stop the drug trade, maybe it would slow it down for a while. Or as Ryan suggested, maybe the doctors did something, or even one of the kids. It could have nothing to do with drugs.

My mind went wild all night. I woke up sweaty, took a shower, changed my gown and went back to bed. When I awoke again, I was as hot and sticky as before.

I showered a second time, put on a robe and sat in a chair to watch Ryan sleep. I took Chili out, fed her and took her to the office with me as I worked. She slept quietly on my lap as I shuffled, wrote, erased, and wrote again, until I had the manuscript the way I wanted it. I was about to put it into the safe when Ryan tapped on the door and opened it. "You're at it early. Have you had breakfast?"

I looked him up and down. He must not have been going to work, he was dressed in faded jeans with one knee almost worn through, a Cardinal's tee-shirt from the 2011 World Series, and loafers with no socks. "I haven't had coffee either. The sooner this task is done, the sooner we won't have to look over our shoulders all the time."

Chili had jumped from my lap and pawed at his leg until he picked her up. "Are you sure it will end there? The Mexican, well, American drug trade is huge. You might go after a bee and wake up the entire hive."

"I know you're worried. I spoke with Roger yesterday and he says when people are caught doing especially heinous deeds, they back off until the publicity dies down."

He tucked Chili under one arm and turned to go. "I've given up trying to get you to stop this. I'll get some coffee and bagels and be back to help you."

"Thanks, but I'm done. I was about to put my finished work in the safe, call Amy and see if she is going to help me with the background checks. But I'm not in such a hurry I can't have breakfast with my two-favorite people."

He walked over and kissed me. Chili, still in his arms, licked both our faces.

Together we made coffee for Ryan and latte for me. He took them to the patio, and I followed with bagels and cream cheese. I looked down at myself. I had on the gown I slept in with one of Ryan's shirts over it. "Maybe I should run and get dressed."

He looked at me thoughtfully. "No one can see us here. Enjoy your breakfast." He went back into the kitchen and returned with apples and orange juice.

The way the house sat on the lot; the morning sun hit the patio. It warmed it nicely before the heat of the day. I picked up my cup just as something whizzed by my head and went straight through the French door into the kitchen sending glass everywhere.

I slid off my seat and on to the concrete under the table. Ryan did the same on his side. Chili tucked herself under me with her tail between her legs. "Where are my men?" Ryan whispered. Before he got it out of his mouth, we heard shouting, two gunshots, and something hitting the fence with enough force to knock a board loose.

Brian, one of the men on guard stuck his face in the open spot and yelled. "You two all right?"

"Yes." Ryan yelled back.

"What do you want us to do with this guy?" Brian said back.

"Bring him in. We'll call the police."

Chili still shook as if she had been out in the cold for hours. Ryan headed to the front door and I jogged up the stairs to get dressed.

I grabbed a pair of wrinkled jeans from the closet floor and reached up to pull a grey tee shirt off a hook. My tennis shoes were by the side of the bed. I sat on the edge to slip them on and noticed Ryan had made the bed before he came downstairs. He was a one of a kind guy.

I combed my unruly hair with my fingers and put it into a low ponytail. The entire thing took all of two minutes. I picked up my phone, tucked my Glock into my jeans at the small of my back, and headed back to the action.

On the way downstairs, I called Roger Simon. Since there were gunshots fired, I doubted it mattered if the police came with sirens or not.

I stepped out to see what had gone on. The people standing around looked like maids, nannies, and gardeners. Most of the residents on the street taught school or were doctors, lawyers and CEOs one place or the other. Not many were stay at home folks, except for the mystery writer who lived four houses down. I didn't see him outside.

Roger and a patrol car were on the way.

On the lawn stood a tall, thin man with an athletic build. No doubt he lifted weights. His muscular thighs strained the material of his pants and his arms barely fit into the jacket sleeves. Blond hair, much too shaggy for my taste, hung over his forehead and curled at the back of his neck. The running shoes he had on I recognized as Nike Vapor Air. They were something he couldn't pick up at the local Wal-Mart. There was nothing about him that shouted, hired thug. He was flanked by two of

Ryan's men.

Ryan pointed to the open door I'd just come through. "Take him inside. We'll wait for Roger before we ask him anything. I don't want to do anything wrong and mess up the case the police will have against him."

Brian and Tommy walked the man inside. They secured his hands behind his back with zip ties and pushed him down onto the couch.

Tommy relayed the story. "Matt and I were in the car out front. This guy came running down the street at a good clip. He stopped, knelt and began to fiddle with his shoe. I saw something drop from his sleeve. We got out of the car to confront him. Matt got there first and the man slugged him. I think he broke Matt's jaw. Before I could get to him, he took off like an Olympic sprinter and headed for the back of the house. He threw the device before I could reach him. Sorry Ryan."

"Sounds like you did it all by the book. Don't be sorry. If we didn't think we might need you, you wouldn't be here. Where's Matt?"

"Johnson drove him to urgent care. The side of his face is a mess. Whatever this guy had in his hand, it cut the hell out of Matt's face."

While they talked about the incident, I went into the kitchen to see what he had thrown with such force it broke a double pane window. It was the size of a roll of quarters. A pin on one side had been pulled, but for some reason it hadn't exploded. I heard the man in the front room say, "I don't want to wait in here. I'd rather wait outside by the curb. You have no right to hold me in here."

I called to Ryan. Brian came with him. "This is some sort of bomb. I can see the timer in red on the side of it. It's set to go off in four minutes."

Ryan looked at Brian. "Go get him." He pointed toward the living room. The timer read three minutes, forty-five seconds.

"What is this?" Ryan asked the man. He shrugged his shoulders.

Brian pushed the man toward the device. "Here, get a closer look." He took a zip tie from a pocket and fastened the man to the table leg.

"What the hell are you doing?" The man jerked as hard as he could to try and break free. The timer read two minutes.

I turned around and picked up Chili. "We are going outside. You can stay here and deal with what you did."

The man's eyes were frantic. "That's murder. You guys will get the needle for this."

Ryan looked down at the bomb. "You've got a minute and a half. In exactly forty seconds, we are all leaving this house, except you."

The man sat horrified now. "Reach in my pocket and get my cell phone. Dial 67, you will hear two clicks, put in 923 and wait until you hear it ring punch 1181. It will shut off."

I did as he said, and the timer stopped with thirty-one seconds to go.

There were so many questions to ask the man. I wished Roger would get here. At that moment, he came in the front door. The first thing he spotted was the bomb. "What's that?"

He nodded to the man who now sagged to the

floor. The only thing holding him up was the restraint around his wrist. I answered for him. "It is a bomb; our friend here was nice enough to shut it down for us."

Captain Simon looked over his shoulder. "Patrolman Floyd, call the bomb squad, tell them to get here yesterday. I've seen these before. Someone can turn it back on as easily as he shut it down."

I looked down. The timer still rested on thirty-one seconds.

Roger took out a note pad and pen from his pocket. "Someone tell me what happened here."

Brian began and related the entire story. Roger told him to release the man from the table leg. I kept my eye on the timer.

Ryan helped the intruder stand on wobbly legs. After a patrolman read him his rights, Roger began to question him. "What's your name?"

"I don't have to tell you," he said defiantly.

"No, you don't. Let me lay out a few facts for you before you decide to be uncooperative. One, you committed an assault. Two, you stand to go down for the attempted murder of these good people and most likely the men outside. Those charges alone will be enough to keep you in prison for the rest of your life. Three, you are a hired goon. The people who hired you would rather you were dead since their little plan didn't work. Going to jail would not be safe for you. And four, I don't like uncooperative people. They make me angry. When I'm angry I tend to exaggerate the severity of the offense. Are you following me?"

Several long seconds passed without a sound in

the room. It only stopped because the bomb squad arrived. They ushered us out of the house and a block down the street.

Roger looked at the bomb thrower and said, "I'm only going to ask one more time. What is your name?"

"August Gillette," the man answered, "and I want a lawyer."

Twenty minutes later the bomb squad came out pushing a hazard box. One of them said to Roger, "We'll take this on the trailer and detonate it at the site. It might be small, but it's mighty."

Patrolman Floyd put August Gillette into the back of his patrol car. Roger followed. Before he left, he said, "I'll be in touch. I can't wait to see who his attorney is."

I called after him. "One more thing, what about the door and damage here?"

He paused. "The CSI team is on its way. Shouldn't take them long to go through it and release your house back to you.

"With your connections Ryan, you should be able to get it fixed by tonight, tomorrow at the latest."

CHAPTER 21

The CSI team came and went within an hour. Ryan called in a favor and a service man was on his way to replace the glass in the side of the French door.

I put Chili in her crate and sat it outside in the shade on the patio. The glass had exploded inward. It covered the floor, table, and counters. In our attempt to clean up enough to survive before a cleaning service got there, we used a broom, damp cloth, and even the vacuum cleaner.

Each time we were sure we had enough cleaned up to let Chili in, Ryan took a flashlight and shined it on the floor. Tiny flecks of glass shimmered back at him.

We didn't have the equipment or know how to remove all the damaged glass. We ordered a pizza, grabbed a couple of soft drinks, and headed outside to keep our little buddy company.

One of Ryan's men came over with cardboard and covered the opening so Chili could be freed from her crate but couldn't go into the house.

The doorbell rang, Ryan went out the backyard gate and walked to the front to retrieve our food. He not only came back with the food, Amy and Nathan were with him. Both were armed.

The people who wanted the story of Ivy Tucker and family to stay secret showed how resourceful they were. No matter how many men, cameras, and security precautions we implemented, the group kept coming with new and different ways to try and stop us.

Nathan had a pizza box in his hand. "Did you bring a pizza? I ordered one a little while ago."

Nathan handed the box to Ryan. "This one is yours; I intercepted the driver out front. I also checked it for bugs. It is spyware free unless they hid it in the cheese."

I walked toward the boarded-up door. "Want a beer?"

Nathan said *yes* as did Ryan. Amy answered, "I'll take a soft drink. I don't want to take any chances with our baby."

Ryan was barefoot. He slipped his loafers off at the door as to not track any glass outside. "You guys stay here and have a seat. I'll go into the war zone and get the drinks and napkins. We planned to eat picnic style. We don't think it is safe to take plates out and set them down on the counter until it is cleaned."

I gave Amy a super-sized hug. "Where's Digger?"

She pointed to Chili's crate. We opened the door so the dog could come and go in the yard. Digger joined her in the bed, and both chewed on treats Amy brought with her.

Ryan came back with several sodas and beer bottles in a small cooler.

Nathan took a long drink of his beer, "The guys said you had another problem over here. Are we going to have to put snipers in the trees to stop this?"

Ryan sat his drink down. "Hum, not a bad idea."

I smiled. "My thought is a large country estate with an alligator filled moat."

Ryan held his bottle and motioned with it. "I think the glass speaks for itself. I'm contemplating my lovely wife's idea, playing duck-and-run has become tiring, and gets more dangerous every day."

I joined Ryan in relaying step-by-step what had happened that afternoon.

My phone rang. It was Roger. "Morris Rainy showed up to represent August Gillette. I should have known. There have always been rumors about him being connected to organized crime and drugs. But lately he has represented every hired man, no matter who is behind it. I wish there was a way to know who his real clients are."

I turned my speaker on, and everyone heard what he said. "Did you question him?"

"No, not yet, that's why I'm calling. Mr. Rainy had a meeting with opposing counsel in another case. Said he'd be back in an hour. If you get here before he does and I can hide you, I thought you might want to listen in."

"Great. We're on our way."

Ryan and I were still dressed in our grungy clothes and didn't take time to change. We each grabbed a piece of pizza to eat on the way. I looked at Ryan. "Think it's all right for me to bring Chili?"

"Don't worry about her," Amy answered. "We'll stay here with her. She and Digger are so happy and content to move now. If they decide to come out of the crate, we can entertain them until you get back."

I ran back and gave Amy a peck on the cheek. "I doubt we'll be long. Two people are coming. A man is on his way to replace the door and one of the companies Ryan uses is coming to clean."

Before we scooted out the door to the garage, Ryan looked back at Nathan. "Be careful and stay armed, better safe than sorry."

Amy and Nathan both waved us on.

The police station hadn't changed in thirty years. It sat seven steps above street level as did most of the buildings downtown. They added a handicap ramp on the front and back otherwise it was the same squat, unattractive brick building with the street number in brick built into the façade.

We parked in the back lot where the police parked their personal cars. The public, including lawyers had to use the front door. It lessened our chances of running into Morris Rainy.

I walked straight to Roger's office, Ryan by my side.

He put us in a small space behind Interrogation Room Two. When I'd been a cop the room was for storing office supplies and items we needed but didn't know what to do with. We had room to sit, stretch our legs and not hit each other's elbows. No claustrophobic could have stayed over a minute in the cramped space. Other than a two-way mirror and a sound system so we could hear the proceedings, the room was bare, and the bile green paint did nothing to make it appealing.

I had interviewed many a suspect in the room we now stared at it through the two-way window.

Roger walked into the empty room. A patrolman escorted Mr. Gillette in shortly after. He was fitted with arm and leg chains.

The attorney arrived last. "Let's get this misunderstanding straightened out. Mr. Gillette would like to sleep in his own bed tonight. Wouldn't you, August?"

The man nodded.

Roger remained silent. He turned on a recording device and TV and gave a stern look at the man who sat next to his Dapper Dan lawyer. "August Gillette, is that your correct name?"

August answered. "August Westfield Gillette."

Roger— "How old are you, August?"

They went on with the preliminary questions for about twenty minutes. Then Roger asked, "What took you to the Mead home this afternoon?"

"Nothing, I went jogging. My shoe came untied and when I stopped to tie it, two men accosted me."

"I need their names," the lawyer said. "We will be filing suits against them for assault."

Roger glanced at Raney but said nothing.

Roger — "Where did you get the bomb you threw into the Meade's home?"

August— "I didn't throw a bomb. I didn't have a

bomb."

Rainy— "What proof do you have that my client threw the bomb or even had it in his possession?"

Roger glared at the lawyer. "Because he defused it when he realized he might blow up with it and his victims."

Rainy looked toward Gillette.

Roger turned his full attention to the subject. "Let's get to the point. You threw an incendiary device into the Meade home. You wanted it to explode. Who hired you to do that?"

August looked at Rainy. "I didn't know the man. He gave me money to throw the thing on the back patio. I threw it too hard and it landed in the house."

Roger — "How much did the man pay you?"

August again deflected to his lawyer.

Rainy — "Tell them."

August— Ten thousand dollars."

Roger— "You want me to believe a stranger gave you that much money to throw something onto a patio."

August— "It's the truth."

Roger— "Then how did you know how to shut the bomb down?"

August— "I guessed."

Kate turned to Ryan. "This is ridiculous. I just want to know who hired him."

"Roger will get to that," Ryan answered.

The interrogation went on another thirty minutes with Roger asking and August giving ridiculous answers.

Then, I could tell, having worked as Roger's partner for seven years, he'd had enough.

Roger— "Let's cut to the chase. I want the name and description of the man who hired you. I want to know if he gave you the device and why he said he wanted you to throw it on the Meade's patio. You are looking at charges of attempted murder, misuse of a deadly weapon, and terrorism. And oh yes, assault for the man's jaw you broke. Your best bet is to co-operate. If you don't, I think you are looking at a long prison stay, maybe the rest of your life."

Morris Rainy leaned over and whispered in August Gillette's ear. Gillette nodded and began to speak. "I work at the Dancing Springs Day Spa, I'm a trainer. Hundreds of people visit there each month. One night I was at Mucho Taco and a man I knew from the spa came in. He said he needed a white guy to play a joke on his friends.

"I knew it wasn't a joke when he offered me ten thousand dollars. My mom is sick, and I thought the money might help her out. I said yes."

Roger asked. "Who constructed the bomb? What did the man look like, or better yet, what was his name?"

"He told me his name was Michael Smith."

Roger tapped his fingers on the table. "Why did he say he needed a white guy? Sounds like he was a white guy."

"No sir, he looked to be Hispanic."

"Let me get this straight. A man belongs to your gym by the name of Michael Smith. He gave you ten grand to throw a bomb onto the Meade's patio as a joke, is that your story?"

Morris Rainy leaned back in his chair and smiled

at Roger. "Sounds like the man you are really after is gone."

Roger turned his attention to the attorney. "Why would you think he was gone? I have the man I want. I have the man who assaulted Mr. Meade's employee, the man who threw the bomb, the man who defused said bomb. I don't need to have the name of the other man to have a solid case against your client."

Rainy turned red. "I'd like to have a word with my client alone, without your tape recorder and monitor."

Roger didn't say anything. He stood, turned off both machines, looked at his watch and said, "I'll be back in five minutes."

There might not have been a recorder on in the room yet Rainy sat directly facing Gillette and talked in a low voice. No matter how hard we tried to watch and listen, we didn't hear a word. We sat back down when Roger went back into the room.

Morris Rainey turned toward August Gillette. "Don't say anything else to these people. I mean nothing. I will take care of the matter we discussed and," he patted August Gillette on the shoulder. "Mr. Gillette is ready to tell you the entire truth now."

He began. "One of my cousins was Dennis Romano. When Kate Nash and her sister broke up the DeMarco family a few years back, it cost Dennis his life. I was getting revenge.

"I got the plans for the little bomb off the Internet and carried out my plan. I'm responsible for everything."

"Mr. Gillette," Roger said, "that all happened years ago, why are you just now moving on your plan to kill Kate and Ryan Meade?"

"I got nothing else to say."

Roger pushed a button under the table, the door opened, and a patrol officer walked in. "Take Mr. Gillette to central booking. Charge him with everything I have noted on this sheet. Put him in a holding cell. I'll be by to sign the charges in a few minutes." Roger stood. "I think we are done here." He hesitated a bit, leaned over; put both hands on the table and got within an inch of the suspect's face. "I'd be very careful if I were you. My guess is that your lifespan is no longer than a few days, He looked at Rainy. "Right, Morris?"

August Gillette sat still. I could see his chest move, and we watched the color drain from his face.

I thought, *he's a dead man,* and he wouldn't have time to spend the money.

As they walked out the door, Roger said, "Only the truth can save you, August Gillette. But I doubt you will have much time to tell it."

CHAPTER 22

Roger Simon left the room and came to us. "You have done a lot of dangerous things in your life, Kate Nash, but this one might be your last. You are getting in the way of millions, probably billions of dollars that flow from South America to here and Canada. Perhaps it goes all around the world from this one gang. Are the lives of the Tucker family, who have been long gone and forgotten more important to you than your own life, and perhaps the lives of Ryan and your friends?"

"If we all thought like you how would the drug traffic and killing ever stop? Besides, we think it might be something totally unrelated to drugs."

Roger looked at Ryan. "Talk to your wife, I have become very fond of her over the years and I don't think she grasps the enormity and the reach of the people she is dealing with. And if you don't think it is drugs or sex trafficking or something equally horrific and dangerous—Kate, you have become naïve."

I knew my temper could blow any minute. I took a deep breath and looked from one man to the other but directed my comments to my old friend and partner. "Those people might be dead; they might not be. Ivy wasn't. I want the people involved in this punished. The Tucker family deserves that much. So far as stopping drug trade, I'm not naïve. I know drugs are the number one suspect here, but if so many people are getting rich by selling drugs, it will never stop. Once I release the book, there will be no reason for anyone to want to hurt me."

Ryan put a hand on each of my shoulders. "I hope you're right about that, my dear."

On the way home I glanced toward Ryan; he focused on the road and had such a grip on the steering wheel his knuckles were white.

We went into the house by way of the garage. No barking dogs greeted us, and my heart sank. So much had happened lately, silence scared me. We quickened our step.

A man in a Remington Windows and Doors shirt was hard at work. He had the new glass in and had been cleaning it with window cleaner and a rag when we reached him. Ryan tapped the man on the shoulder and he visibly jumped. "Sorry sir, wondering where our family is?"

He pointed to the back yard. I looked out. I had no idea they would stay outside. I could tell the cleaning crew had come and gone, not a sliver of glass in sight and an invoice lay on the table.

Amy and Nathan were lying on a blanket at the

far end of the yard. They looked to be asleep and each had a dog resting on their chest.

The worker packed up his tools and said, "If there is nothing else, I'll be going."

Ryan walked him to the door and must have given him a tip for missing part of his Sunday to repair our French door. The man sounded extremely happy when he left.

We each grabbed a bottle of water and went out to the yard as quietly as possible. It didn't help. The minute the dogs smelled or heard us, they scampered off the sleeping couple and made a beeline for us.

Amy and Nathan turned over, raised their bodies on their elbows and looked at us. They both lay down again. What a beautiful, lazy afternoon.

Ryan had not said a word to me since we left the police station. We sat at the patio table; I put my hand on his. "Are you ever going to talk to me?"

He turned my way and smiled. "Thinking about August Gillette. Do you think someone hired him to bomb us? Or is he part of the cartel? Whoever hired him trusted him enough to send him to the house and disarm the bomb."

"I didn't give it much thought but now that you bring it up, someone thinks enough of him not to let him blow himself up. In the crime culture, that's a big deal."

"I'm sure his bail will be paid tomorrow and no one will ever see him again for one of two reasons. Either he'll end up floating in the muddy Mississippi for his ineptness or whisked away to a safe location the authorities don't know about."

I took my hand away, unscrewed the cap on my water bottle and took a drink. "What bothers me the most is to them everyone is disposable. Me, you, those two," I pointed to our friends who seemed to have gone back to sleep in the spring sun. "Even their own families or other people's families, all for money. What have we, as a people, become?"

He put his hand on mine. "If we're going to do this, let's get it done, now. I want to send Amy and Nathan and Digger on a trip. I'll send them on a company plane. I don't have a plan yet, but we'll create some sort of diversion so no one notices they're gone until it is too late to track them."

"Do you think it's possible?"

"Anything's possible."

A half an hour later our friends joined us on the patio. Amy said, "I guess that was rude. It has been a long time since I've been so relaxed and calm."

Ryan pulled two chairs out from under the table and motioned for them to sit. "We didn't consider it rude. Had the blanket been larger, we might have joined you. We need to talk to you about something," he continued. "We didn't learn anything downtown except the man who threw the bomb is connected. Otherwise he wouldn't have been able to afford his high-priced attorney, and they would have let him die with us in the house. I reached down to pick up Chili who jumped at my leg.

Amy spoke up. "Maybe we have approached this from the wrong point of view. How do we know the Tucker's didn't tick someone in Chicago off bad enough to kill them? Maybe the kids were collateral damage."

Ryan leaned forward and put his hands on his knees. "You're right. We should take a longer and closer look in that direction. Meanwhile, we'd like to send you two on a vacation far from here until this is over."

Amy looked at Nathan and then at me. "And you believe once the book is released, the danger will end?"

Kate answered. "Actually, I do. As we talked about before, those people don't want notoriety. Once the story comes out and the publicity blossoms, it will all die down. Once they're bombarded with it, they'll crawl back into their holes. The challenge is to stay safe until then."

Nathan put both hands on the table. "And you think the answer to the two of us remaining safe is to leave our home, our garden, our jobs, and run off somewhere leaving our dog."

The next few minutes were dead still.

Ryan spoke up. "When you put it like that, it seems you're getting punished for being our friends. Tell us what you'd like."

Amy put a hand on Nate's knee. "I want to live as I do and not have to worry about this drama. I understand why you want to do it, and we have decided to help, we're wiser than we were before." She nodded at Ryan. "With your help, I'm sure we can all stay safe, but we're living at our own home. Tomorrow, we're picking up a new dog. She's well trained and able to see and hear things we can't."

I asked. "Are you sure about this?"

"Yes, we are," they answered together.

Ryan tried to lighten the mood. "Tell us about your new dog."

Nathan stood. "Mind if I go inside and get me and my lady a drink first?"

I jumped to my feet so fast I almost lost Chili from my lap. "Geez, I'm sorry. What can I get you?"

We all went inside and talked. Before we uttered a sentence, Amy put her finger to her lips. She acted like she was writing on a piece of invisible paper. Ryan went to a kitchen drawer and came back with the grocery list pad and a pen. Amy wrote. *"Did you check for bugs? Something doesn't feel right."*

"I have the disrupter on," Ryan mouthed. "He sat a second before he and Nathan scrambled, each in a different direction. Ryan headed for our new office and came back with a wand. Nathan drew his gun and disappeared out the back door and then the gate. He came back with a scanner, sat it on the counter, put on a set of headphones, and began to turn dials and press buttons.

Amy and I sat quietly and watched the show. An hour later, there were seven listening devices of different types stacked next to me on the table.

Ryan had found three and Nathan, four more. I put them in a colander, sat them inside the dishwasher and turned it on the heavy setting.

I turned back to the other three. "So much for these little gadgets." I put the deflector on the table. I'm beginning to think the idea of a well-trained dog is marvelous. Tell us about him."

"Her," Amy said. "The trainer suggested since Digger is a boy, we should get a female. Sally is a big dog and we don't want to take a chance on her hurting our little boy."

Ryan said, "You've never told us what kind of dog."

Nathan laughed. "She's a two-year-old Rottweiler. She had a seasoned trainer, she's a personal protection dog, a real charmer. If you take her for a walk and say potty, she leaves the path, squats, and is back in a flash. When someone walks by, she becomes super alert. The man who delivered her to the kennel here said she is one of the best. They are trained near Quantico by off duty FBI trainers."

I wasn't a lover of big dogs. Chili was my first dog and the only pet I'd ever had. A Rottweiler would terrify me, even if it was mine. "If we wanted to adopt a dog, we should get a male?"

Amy answered. "According to what they told us. I was afraid because one bite and Digger would be gone. They showed us videos of Sally letting a baby bite her ears and kittens sleeping on her back. And Digger is getting older. He's nine now, he's pretty laid back."

I glanced toward Chili who had just run to the bedroom and back several times at top speed as she tried to get Digger to chase her. Nothing laid back about her. Of course, she was only three.

Amy continued. "Talk to them. We will get you our contact. I bet they recommend a German Sheppard. They are good with other dogs."

"Do you think Sally would be okay with Chili playing with the two of them?"

"You'll see," Nathan said. "She is a great dog. I

don't think we would have had near as many problems to date with bugs and break-ins if we'd had a well-trained dog. I guarantee whoever planted those bugs while we were napping in the yard would never have been able to if Sally had been here."

Ryan and I looked at one another. He went to get refills on our drinks. "I don't know why I didn't think of it. We use Hobo every day. One of the guys checks out the security system with the dog. I hadn't put two and two together."

Amy leaned forward and petted Digger, who sat at her feet. "Think about it. Many people have a dog instead of a gun. If they are trained not to take treats from strangers, it is safe for them. It is proven a criminal will kill a person before he will kill a dog."

So would I, I thought.

For the next three weekends, Ryan and I took Chili with us and went dog shopping. Six dogs were introduced to us as perfect matches. On the last day, we chose an eighteen-month-old black and tan German Sheppard named Axel. Axel loved Chili. I just hoped Sally, Digger, Chili, and Axel got along.

A retired Army trainer brought her to the house. We all went for a walk, me with Chili, Ryan leading Axel, and our trainer pointing out all of Axle's many talents.

On the third night, we all walked to the Loop. This time I had the new dog and Ryan had Chili. She heeled the entire time until we got into a crowd by the movie theater as at least thirty people came out the doors. She blocked my way and sat in front of me. When a clear path became visible, she walked back to my side and continued our stroll. He performed perfectly and I didn't have to worry about anyone touching me. Most folks cut a wide birth around her although she paid no attention to them.

On the way home, a man bumped into Ryan. Axel pushed Ryan back and jumped on the man with his two front feet on the guys shoulders. He bared his teeth although he didn't hurt the man, who yelled, *it was an accident. Please, call off your dog.*

I did. The dog stayed an inch or two from the man and growled. I turned to Jason, the trainer. "Should I call the police?"

"No, Mr. and Mrs. Meade, this is David. He volunteered to bump into you so you could get a picture of what to expect."

Ryan shook the man's hand. "Nice to meet you."

We stood and talked for about five minutes. Before they left, the trainer said, "I think you have yourselves a personal protection dog. I know she'll be all you want and more."

CHAPTER 23

The next day, Amy and I talked about The Kate Nash Detective Agency. "After the three big cases we've been involved with, I was bored when we did the short-changer. I could hardly wait until it was over."

Amy reached down to pet Sally who laid on the floor with Digger, spread out comfortably on the big dog's back. "I know what you mean. Remember when we went from one case to the next, perfectly satisfied? I think we should turn our office's day to day work to Marsh and Marsh."

Chili kept trying to get Axel to take a toy and play with her. Axel put his paw gently on Chili's head and licked her. "Is that the two brothers who are retired military?" I asked.

"I don't think I told you about these men. The father was on the force with me in Chicago. He retired early and moved down here to be near his son when his wife died. They want to open an agency. I've been sliding work over to them ever since we began this case and the background checks. Nathan is not cut out to be a helper. He just won't say no to Ryan."

I looked around the office. "I don't think we need the Clayton office anymore. We have everything we need right here. We could find an interesting unsolved murder or robbery and see if the victims or their families would like to hire us."

Amy said, "Or they will fall in our lap like this one did."

"We aren't making any money on this one."

"Kate, I bet when we put *The Untimely Death of Ivy Tucker* out, money will come in."

I laughed. "It didn't cross my mind, you're probably right."

We sat and looked at one another for a long time. "Well?" she finally said. "What do you think?"

I picked up Chili. "Let's meet with the Marsh men. I want to like the people we turn the agency over to. We are selling it to them, right? Meanwhile, I have a present for you."

I opened the desk drawer and handed her a box. She opened it. "Oh, my, "she said, "I didn't expect this."

They were business cards but instead of the old ones that read Kate Nash Agency and at the bottom, Amy Perkins Associate, they now said Nash & Perkins Detective Agency and had her name and mine at the bottom as associates. "Ryan rented us a post office box, so people won't come to the house. We could go to them. The box number is 1313".

She laughed. "In honor of your favorite childhood show, The Monsters," I said.

Amy beamed. "Are you ready to get started on the book?"

"No," I answered. "Something Ryan said got me to thinking. Maybe the neighbor Mrs. Caulfield wasn't as she seemed. And why did the Donnellson's want to be our best friends at the whaling camp? There were others there much more friendly than we were and more their age."

Amy and I had gone to the kitchen to get a snack and a cool drink. I wasn't quite used to Axel dogging my every step. Chili still required as much lap time as she could con out of me.

Sally stayed with Amy the same way. Digger, who liked floor time more than Chili, walked squarely under Sally's belly. The Rottweiler didn't seem to notice or the fact that Digger liked to lay between her front legs anytime she lay down, or better yet, on her back. Amy and Nathan had taken a million pictures. I prayed the dog liked the new baby.

Amy looked up from watching her two dogs. "It's a small world. It's difficult to say with certainty how many people were involved in the Tucker family's disappearance."

While she talked, I'd been fixing us each a tuna salad sandwich with Havarti cheese, a side of carrot sticks, chips, and fresh pineapple for dessert. "My, my," Amy commented as I pushed the plate in front of her. Aren't we getting healthy?"

She popped a chip in her mouth and said, "Okay, after lunch, let's start with the Tuckers' neighbor."

Axel always lay right outside the room, but far enough to the side, people could come and go. So long as I didn't get upset, she slept peacefully. The phone rang. I listened intently. Before the person hung up, Amy came in. "You aren't going to believe this. The biggest newspaper in the country wants to do a serial on our book. They offered me a huge sum of money. When I said the money wasn't important, he laughed."

Amy leaned forward in her chair. "How did they find out about it?"

"Apparently, my friend went to a publisher's forum in New York and told the paper about it. He said it was the kind of story they hunt for but never find."

"Kate, we are going to be famous." She didn't sound happy.

"I'm already famous, or infamous is more like it. It is not all it is cracked up to be.

"I have an idea," I said, "let's make up two names and use them, you know, a nom de plume."

"What if we have to make an appearance?"

"We can put that off until after the people in question are in custody."

I stood and stretched. "I feel like two gals who just won the lottery and are dreaming about what to do with the money."

I walked to the printer. Chili wanted me to pick her up. I kept telling her to *wait a minute*. I couldn't take my eyes off the paper the computer spit out. After the third reading I leaned back in my chair and read it out loud.

Mrs. Martha Caulfield, 1918 Moss Land Drive,

Chicago, was found dead in her home on July 11, 2009. Mrs. Caulfield's daughter called local police for a wellness visit when her mother didn't answer the door. Mrs. Caulfield, age 91, died of natural causes.

Amy stood behind me to read over my shoulder. "Who was the so called neighbor who talked to you and Ryan?"

"I have no idea, but how did she know we were coming to visit and why did she go to so much trouble to lie to us? "

Amy perched on the corner of my desk. "When I was with the police force up there, I had a good friend, Stan Russell. I'll call and see if he'll go over to the house and see what he can find out."

"Oh, Amy, do you think he will go?"

"Sure, I do. If you'll take the dogs out to potty, I'll give him a call now."

"So, he is the sort of friend you don't want to talk to with me in the room." Her face turned the color of the red tank top she wore. "Come on, guys," I said to all four dogs. "Let's give Miss Secretive some privacy."

Digger, Chili, and Axel walked to me and began to follow. Sally, on the other hand, went to Amy and sat in a heel position and waited. "She won't leave me. I'll meet you outside after I talk to Stan."

I gave her a bigger smile and went off with my parade of canine.

When Amy and Sally joined us, Sally waited for the command to go romp with the other dogs. Romp might not have been the correct word. Axel laid stretched on his side. Digger and Chili took turns walking over him. He didn't twitch an ear.

"Stan says he's off today and will drive over and look. It will take him a couple of hours, his wife is having an ultrasound, and he doesn't want to miss the first view of baby number two.

"Meanwhile, I didn't get a chance to tell you what I found. Eric Tucker had three partners. They shared in everything equally. Before the family left for their vacation, he sold his share to the other three for $1.4 million and had the money sent to an offshore account in the Cayman Islands.

"I have no way of finding out whose name the account is in.

"None of the other doctors had anything bad to say about him. The staff at the practice said they were all shocked to find out Dr. Tucker was leaving the practice. He gave no concrete reason why. He let them believe he wanted to retire and spend time with his family. No one had reason to question him."

"Wow. This changes everything. Where did you get the information?"

We were back in the office which we decided to name, *The Tomb*, because on the inside it was as quiet as one. "This time instead of talking to the general employees, I talked to his Physician's Assistant and his nurse of seventeen years. It must have been a secret because until the day he left, everyone but the partners believed he would be back in a few months.

"The amount of money he received from his liquidation was filed in court. I searched it on public records."

"I don't know, Amy; I think we have been barking up the wrong tree. It certainly doesn't sound as if he planned to go home after his vacation."

"I know. I've put everything we know about Sharon Tucker in the computers. They are working on it now."

Amy's phone rang. "Hi Stan, what did you find out?" She began to take notes and after her initial question, all Kate heard was, Huh, really, no kidding, amazing, Mr. Nelson, ok, got it, thanks." She swiveled her chair toward me. "This just keeps getting better and better. Mr. Nelson, the neighbor two doors down bought the Tuckers' home before they left. What was important to them and the kids, they put in a storage locker and paid two years rent.

"Mr. Homer Nelson made the house into an AIRBNB. The lady who greeted you as Martha Caulfield rented the house for three nights. He can't tell us anything more about her other than her name, if it is her real name. She paid the rent and fees in cash."

"Stan said the owner showed him the paperwork on her stay and the driver's license and passport. Her name is Christine Hampton, age 45, her address is listed as Ashland, Texas."

My phone rang, it was Ryan. "There is a play tonight in Webster Groves, Shakespeare in the Park Series. The program is Rent. I thought since the nights have been so cool, we could grab a couple of lawn chairs and go."

This would be tough. My head had been wrapped around the case for months. We'd had no normal life and I knew it would lift his spirits. I wanted nothing more than to stay where I was and keep going now that the floodgates started to open. I took a deep breath. "Sounds like fun. I assume it's casual. What about Axel and Chili? Is it a picnic sort of thing? Do I need to fix something? Okay, what time is it now? My goodness, I'll stop what I'm doing and get dressed. See you in a few."

A minute after I hung up Nathan called Amy. I leaned back in my chair, crossed my arms, and listened to an almost exact conversation as the one I had with Ryan.

She stood. "No use going over this with you. I'd better get these dogs home, shower, feed them, and be excited about this evening when Nathan gets home. I'll see you at six-thirty at the Root Beer Stand."

The dogs and I walked her to her car and waved goodbye. The things I did for love. Then I chastised myself. I had everything a woman could want and a loving husband. I should never make light of it.

I went in, locked the front door behind me and fed the dogs in the kitchen. They followed me upstairs while I picked out a peach colored tee with a scoop neck and a pair of teal Capri's with flowers the color of my shirt.

Axel lay outside the bathroom door as I showered.

The next voice I heard was Ryan's. "Are you almost done in there or can I join you?"

I stepped out of the bathroom wrapped in two spa towels, one around my body and another around my head. "Ten minutes earlier and this would all have turned out differently."

He laughed and glanced over his shoulder at the bedside clock. He looked back to me, smiled and shrugged his shoulders. "Sorry I didn't call sooner. Michael White dropped by with the tickets and looked as though he would be offended if we didn't take him up on it. His wife plays Maureen."

I walked over and kissed him. "It sounds like fun. You'd better get ready. We need to meet Amy and Nathan in an hour."

One of Ryan's men had four chairs set up for us when we arrived. We got some odd looks when Axel and Sally walked beside us. No one saw the little guys. They were in their carriers during the entire performance.

No one offered to pet the two big dogs. Without being told, one of them laid behind the chairs and faced away from the stage. The other one lay in front of the chairs facing the stage. After the first act, I relaxed. Unless someone hunted us with a long-range sniper rifle, no one could hurt us. I wondered if the other playgoers noticed the men strategically placed around the park, in dark suits and bulges under their jackets.

I didn't realize how much we needed a night out without the Tuckers following us. By the time we left the park, we were relaxed and chatting about how much Amy and Nathan enjoyed their yard and outside in general.

Amy had a baby bump and Nathan took care of her as though she would break. We were all in a hurry to go to our own homes. We said our good-byes in the parking lot. I realized on the way home I held my breath. Ryan broke my train of thought. "A penny for your thoughts."

"Nothing really. I keep waiting for something to happen. It's been a long time since we had a non-eventful evening."

"Kate don't jinx it. A lot has to do with the new dogs." He laughed before he said, "Did you see the other people walk around us in a circle much bigger than needed to stay away from them? I don't know which one they fear the most, to me, Sally looks the most ferocious."

"I wouldn't want either one of them mad at me."

We pulled into the garage and Ryan unlocked the kitchen door. Axel went in, and after a few minutes, he came back to us, sat, and barked one time, indicating the house was secure.

I smiled. I loved it.

The Tent Theater Event made for an early evening. We were home, sitting around in comfy clothes with a glass of wine by ten. It felt good to have nothing to do for a few hours.

Ryan caught me up on his work. "I would like to utilize a few drones. There's a place in Manitoba called The Sky Spies. I want to go up next week, meet them and make sure I know what I'm doing."

"Does that mean you will replace men with drones?"

"Kate, you know I wouldn't do that. It's a safety net for my guys. Last week, two men sneaked in the lot at Can Co Pharmacy Distribution. James and Benny did a great job stopping them, but spent two hours chasing them down, waiting for the police to arrive and get back to their posts. It left the warehouse unguarded.

"A drone could have tracked the thief and know exactly where he was when the police arrived. The men don't wear uniforms and I'm always afraid one could get shot.

"Would you like to go to Canada with me?"

I moved closer to him which isn't always easy with Chili between us. "I'd love to but knowing Eric Tucker never planned to go back to Chicago has got my imagination on overload. Tomorrow we are going to check into how Sharon left her practice."

"Maybe they knew their family was in danger and wanted to get far away."

He picked up Chili in one arm and extended his other hand to me. "Let's take these critters outside and go upstairs. I'm tired and my plane leaves at seven which means I have to be at the airport at five."

"What am I missing here?" I asked. "You're going out of town and leaving me in the care of Axel? I believe he can handle it, but I still can't believe you even considered it."

Axel picked up her ball and nudged Ryan's hand for him to throw it. He did, so, of course, Chili and I had to play tug-o-war.

Once we made it upstairs, Ryan said, "I really do think the dog can take care of you, but since we haven't tested him out yet, I have two of my men standing guard. They'll be over to meet Axel in the morning, so they'll still have all their limbs when I get back. I sent a text to your private cell number with the password."

I laughed and said, "I know, if they don't know the passwords, shoot them."

CHAPTER 24

D r. Sharon Tucker sold her portion of her practice also. She had one partner, a Dr. Kenneth York. According to the disillusionment papers, her portion was well over a million dollars." I told Amy.

She came to stand behind me and look over my shoulder. "Does it say how the money was paid?"

"It says it was a cash settlement. We both know what that means. The money could be anywhere."

Amy put her hand up to her mouth and gasped. "Maybe the money was in the boat. It would have been motive to rob and murder the Tuckers."

I turned farther around so I didn't have to strain my neck. "I thought of that too, but where was the money? If Ivy's pictures of the happening are correct, which we have assumed they are, why would the man burn the boat?"

"Maybe the money wasn't in the boat at that

point. Maybe he stowed it in the dinghy, and someone found out, so he had to kill them," she said.

I relaxed in my chair. "Okay. Let's make a list of everything we know."

Amy chose a desk, turned on the computer, put her hands on the keyboard. "I'm ready."

When we were finished, we each read it over.

Both Doctors Tucker sold out their partnerships, kept it quiet, and let everyone think they were going on vacation.

They had the children's permanent school records.

They sold the house, cars, and gave the furnishings to charity. The things they cared about were in a storage locker prepaid for two years.

The woman next door died years before and a Christine Hampton of Ashland, Texas pretended to talk to us and most likely did it to reinforce the story of the family vacation.

If we believed Ivy's drawings, someone on the boat killed everyone but her. The logical person to be the murderer would have been the captain, Michael Mannes.

According to Maria, Ivy stayed with her and her niece for ten years until she decided to leave.

At which time, she was murdered, and murdered with something leading to Mexico.

Someone attacked you and Nathan and me and Ryan and threatened to throw us off track.

I made a copy for each of us. We both stared at the bullet points until one of the dogs whined, and we realized they wanted to go outside.

After I alerted the men on guard what we were going to do, we stopped by the kitchen for a cold drink and headed for the patio.

We didn't talk for a long while. The dogs let us know they were ready to go in. Each took a drink of cold water from the bowls on the floor and followed us to The Tomb.

At almost the same time, we both said we thought we should find out more about Christine Hampton. We ran her through all our databases. She had no criminal record. There was no record of anyone by her name that ever lived in Ashland, Texas. We ran her driver's license number through the DMV. It came back as belonging to ninety-five-year-old Marci Dodd of Dallas. She died three years earlier.

"There is no reason to pursue her further. Before we stop, let's see if she has a past in the Chicago area.". The first button I pushed brought up a story about Christine, her son, Levi, and her husband John. I read it out loud.

Three-year-old Levi Hampton drowned in the family swimming pool on Sunday, June 7, 1999. A neighbor, Dr. Eric Tucker, a pediatrician from Midland Hospital was the first one on the scene and said he did all he could for the child.

Dr. Tucker pronounced the boy dead before the ambulance arrived. Mrs. Hampton had to be sedated when she wouldn't stop screaming that Dr. Tucker never liked the boy and didn't try hard enough and long enough to save him.

Midland coroner agreed with Doctor Tucker that nothing else could have been done for the boy.

An autopsy confirmed Levi had been in the water over thirty minutes before his father found him.

Amy patted her stomach. "How horrible. Apparently, Mrs. Hampton blamed Eric Tucker for the boy's death. I wish I knew why he was alone by the pool."

"I'll dig deeper," I said. "Here's something else."

John Robert Hampton was found dead this morning. Mr. Hampton was the father of little Levi Hampton, age 3, who drowned in the family's backyard swimming pool. The investigation of Levi Hampton's accidental death pointed to his father John.

At the time of the accident, Mrs. Hamilton blamed her next-door neighbor Dr. Eric Tucker for the boy's death saying he didn't try everything he could to save the boy.

His father was supposed to swim with Levi and not leave him in the pool alone. John became interested in a baseball game and went inside to get a beer.

Mr. Hamilton said he didn't know how much time had passed before he realized the boy was floating face down in the water.

Friends and family said John Hamilton was a loving and devoted father who became distracted.

Although authorities haven't released the suicide note Mr. Hampton left, they say he felt solely responsible for his son's death and couldn't live with the guilt. Mrs. Hampton, who is under a doctor's care, did not comment.

"We need to delve further into the Hamiltons. I mean Mrs. Hamilton. She could have something to do with all of this."

Amy shook her head. "Surely not. It sounds as if it was a horrible accident."

We went back three years before Levi Hamilton's death and scoured the papers for articles we could find with Christine Hamilton, Eric Tucker, and Sharon Tucker, in the same article.

Several came up with the desired criteria. "The problems with the Hamiltons all took place in Glencoe. When the Tuckers left the area to go wherever they were going they lived in Long Grove. I'm guessing they moved because of the tragedy that happened in the neighborhood.

"Before the date of the drowning, John Hamilton filed a boundary dispute stating the Tuckers' driveway sat mostly on his property. It says here the case was settled out of court for an unspecified amount of money."

"They had trouble long before Levi's death," Amy said.

"A year later, Christine ran over the Tuckers' dog. One of the neighbors said she veered to the other side of the street to hit him." I looked at Amy. "How many stories have you read over the years where two families can't get along and act like small children?"

"What was the outcome of the incident?"

"The Tuckers did not press charges. They went before the Neighborhood Association and got permission to fence a part of their yard for the dog. According to this story, it was a long hard fight."

Amy asked, "Why didn't the Tucker family move?"

"They did after the last confrontation. It says here Christine put signs on the Tuckers' lawn. Baby Killer, Sharon Tucker is an illegal. They sold the house and moved to the house Ryan and I went too. Amazing. Maybe she is behind all of this."

Digger and Chili began to demand attention. Amy picked them up, one in each arm. "It would destroy me if someone hurt one of these dogs." She motioned with her head to encompass all four dogs. "Let's take a moment. This is all too emotional for me. Maybe because I'm pregnant. I just want to cry."

"Okay. I'm going to text the guys outside and offer them something to drink. Ryan has them on twelve-hour shifts to make sure no one bothers me, as if Axel would let anyone get near me."

The men were thrilled to get a cold drink. Ryan told them to order lunch and not to leave their posts. One Coke or iced tea from a fast food restaurant wouldn't be enough for a big man in the heat.

He also wanted them in their Meade clothes. Today it was tan polo shirts with the company logo, dark brown khakis, and of course, they were armed.

Amy and I played with the dogs. Axel loved his belly rubbed, as did Sally. Of course, Digger and Chili had been the most spoiled dogs ever since birth.

I looked at the clock. "It's after five. Are you ready to call it a day?"

"I'm torn," she said. "If we stop now, I won't be able to get the case off my mind. When will Ryan be home?"

"Thursday. If you are worried about me, don't

be. The men who come on at seven will be in the house. You know Ryan. He has it well fool proofed. I know Bobby and Randy who will be here tonight. Still, if they don't know the correct passwords, I'm supposed to shoot them."

It was the first time we laughed all day.

My phone rang. "Kate, Nathan is outside. I know this seems strange but if we don't follow every one of Mr. Meade's instructions, he'll go ballistic."

"Put him on," I said. "Hi Nathan, what's your password?"

"Babies with red hair," he answered and came in. "I know you two ladies think Ryan has gone overboard," he said as he closed the door behind him. "As Ryan explained it to me, it is discipline. One shortcut could get someone killed. It's rare we watch one of our own."

Digger jumped at his leg, Sally sat next to him and Amy put her hand on his arm. "We know, honey. I'm a better-safe-than-sorry-gal myself."

"Are you ladies down for the night?"

I pointed to Amy. "She and I learned some sad and disturbing facts today. Your lady needs a couple of hours of fresh air in the garden. The last thing we want to do is think about this case all night."

Amy gave me a hug. "Promise me you will not work on it any more today."

"I promise. Bobby is bringing Chinese takeout. I'll probably play hearts with them for a bit, take a hot bath and curl up with a book I've been trying to find time to read. Go home, don't worry about me. I'll see you in the morning, Amy. Bye Nathan."

The evening remained uneventful. Bobby was the best Hearts player I had ever encountered, and I reminded myself never to get into a poker game with him.

I had great intentions of beginning a book, but once I took a long hot bath, I was ready for bed. With no hesitation what-so-ever, Axel jumped up on the end of the bed and stretched out horizontally. Chili took her usual spot under the covers.

CHAPTER 25

I dressed and took the dogs downstairs to go out for their morning ritual. The smell of fresh brewed coffee whiffed up at me as I descended the stairs.

The men had changed shifts, Danny took the dogs out and Roger poured me a cup of coffee. I didn't have the heart to tell him I didn't like coffee much. Instead, I loaded the hot brew with French Vanilla Crème and sipped it until Amy arrived.

She brought pastries for all of us. I took a glazed donut and headed for the Tomb. "I was sure I would be up all night thinking about the Tuckers and the Hamiltons, but I went right to sleep. How about you?" I asked.

"We worked on the garden until dark. It is so relaxing. Something about playing in the dirt soothes my soul."

"I feel the same way about the ocean. When I

was a kid, I sat on the beach and let the waves lap at my toes. One year, Mom taught summer school. I had more alone time and made an entire series of stories about what happened under the water. I scared myself so badly I didn't go in the water for a month."

She laughed and picked up the paper about Christine Hamilton. "Why do you think she moved to a tiny place such as Ashland, Texas?"

"I hope we find out today why she moved there. Did she have anything to do with the disappearance of the Tuckers and did she know Michael Mannes?"

Amy turned on her computer. "A better question is why did she meet us at the Tucker house? Where are you going to start? I don't want to do the same searches you do."

"I'm going with My Life."

"Okay. Let's see who's the first to find anything."

All you could hear in the room was dogs breathing and the tapping of computer keys. This went on until Amy pointed to her computer screen. "I found Christine Hamilton's sister. Actually, I found Christine Ford's sister. Her name is Janice Ford Johnston. She lives in Willow Lake, a suburb of Dallas and owns a scuba diving school. *Divine Diving, Janice Johnston, and Dwayne Johnston, Certified Instructors.*"

"I'll run her through CODIS and see what we get." I pecked and hunted for a good ten minutes before the printer spit out the report. "Janice Johnston is fingerprinted because she was in the Navy and retired as a Commander. She has no criminal record, not so much as a speeding ticket. According to this, she is an only child. Do you get the impression we are being led in a big circle?"

Amy stood and stretched. "I'm only four months into this baby thing and I already can't sit for long periods because of my belly. There must be a reason Christine came up with Janice Johnston in our search.?

"Maybe so. Personally, I think someone is yanking our chain. Someone with the clout to doctor files. If they are manipulating records, we may never connect Michael Mannes with anyone else. I wonder if I could blow up the picture of Michael that Ivy drew and send it to the Mexican police to see if they can identify him."

Amy sat again. "I thought the only drawing of him was with a devil's face."

I got up, went to the safe and retrieved the original drawings. "Let's get some magnifying glasses and look at these more closely. You know how it is when you have your mind set something is the way you think it is. It blocks out what might *really* be the truth."

"Let's take the dogs out and put these on the kitchen counter where we can look at them at the same time. Do you have another magnifier?"

"Ryan has one in the kitchen drawer to use on all those little words on labels we can no longer see with the naked eye. Grab the one on the desk over there by you."

Once we had a cold drink. I got the first picture out of the packet and we began to go over it more closely." It's the house they lived in before they left on the trip."

Amy leaned down closer and scoured the picture for anything we might have missed. "I didn't realize before, but all of the shades are drawn. You can see the little knob you use to raise and lower them. Would you close everything up if you planned on coming back?"

I looked up at her. "They didn't have to worry about that. They knew the house was sold and everything of value had been removed. There was no need to make it appear as though someone came and went like we all do when we go on vacation. At that point, I'd say even Ivy knew they were not coming back."

The next picture was one of the Iguana Boat Rental office. There was no mistaking Reginald Saylor as the man we'd met on our trip. Ivy focused her art on the man and counter. The doomed boat could be seen through the window. There was no mistaking the sign on the schooner, Iguana Veloz. "That picture brings forth another question," I said, "I assumed the picture was drawn when they arrived, yet, in this drawing, the boat they had not chosen until they arrived was tied to the dock outside the office window."

Amy smiled at me. "Poetic license."

"You mean maybe Ivy drew her rendition of things and not what actually happened?"

"Could be. She was a twelve-year-old kid. If you put three people in the rental office and let them study it for a half-an-hour, then took them off into separate rooms and questioned each one on what they saw, they would all describe it differently."

The next dozen pictures were not too exciting, we combed every square inch; nothing. Then I saw it. On the first picture of the schooner anchored outside the lagoon entrance, an object appeared in the background we had not noticed before.

We each studied it. "We need a jeweler's loupe," she said. "Do you have one?"

"No, and right now I'm a prisoner in my own home. The guys are not going to let me go out to buy one."

She took her phone from her pocket. I listened to her end of the conversation. "Where are you today, honey? Really? That's great. I need a jeweler's loupe. Oh, Kate just showed me her phone search. It lists Home Depot, Wal-Mart, Harbor Freight, almost anywhere. I understand. Okay, I'll tell them. Thanks, babe, I love you."

"What did he say?"

"He said to tell one of the men outside to call Jacob. He has several of them. Someone from the office will bring it over."

"Get off your feet. I'll text Bobby to come to the door."

Within the hour, we had a 30X loupe. I used it first. "It looks like a ship, far in the background. You can only see the top and part of the side. The rest is low in the water. Something is written on the side. I can pick out W L D T E R. You look while I find something to write on."

I wrote down the letters I could make out. Amy had two more. O T.

Once the letters were put in the correct place, we had WO_ LD T_ _ _ _ _ _ _.

Amy held the etching against the patio door. The light helped us pick out R _ _ _ _ _

Laid out, it read WO_ LD TR_ _ _ _ _ _.

Amy put the picture back flat on the counter. "I feel as if I'm on Wheel of Fortune."

"I hope you are good at it. I think the first word is WORLD."

"I agree, but WORLD what?"

"Treasures," Amy guessed.

"Let's put that expensive hardware to work. We can contact the Coast Guard in the area and see if they can match the second word for us."

Amy picked up the readout as it came out of the printer. "There are seventeen hundred-eighty-nine boats that begin with World. Only two happen to sail in our area of interest, World Dominator and World Travelers. World Travelers is owned by a company out of Dallas, Texas by the name of Divine Diving."

"Janice and Dwayne Johnston own a company named Divine Diving in Dallas. I think we finally have something. We need to find out where it is housed and where it sailed in June of 2004. I don't know about you, but I'm worn out. Nathan will be here any minute. Let's tackle this in the morning."

I stood and so did all four dogs. "That works for me. Ryan will be home tomorrow. Some sleep would be nice."

Bobby called from the porch. "Kate, there is a tall guy out here. He looks familiar but he doesn't have a password. Should I shoot him or let him in?"

Amy opened the door for Nathan.

The shift changed at seven and the new men

came in for the night. I skipped the card game, took a hot shower, talked to Ryan, and went through the facts we uncovered earlier in the day.

I always gained more perspective when I could start at the beginning of my day and go through its events as though they were a movie. My revelation came around three a.m.

Since there were two of Ryan's men, I would have to walk by to go into the Tomb. I slipped on my house shoes and bathrobe before I tiptoed downstairs.

Chili didn't move, she stayed snuggled under the covers at the end of the bed. Axel walked beside me. Michael, the man whose turn it must have been to guard the house looked up at me. In a low voice he asked, "Everything copasetic, Mrs. Meade?"

I didn't believe three-twenty in the morning the proper time to correct him, so I gave him an okay sign and kept walking.

There was no way I could sleep until I looked at the picture Ivy Tucker drew of the night the boat burned, and her conception of her surroundings while she floated until she nearly died.

I found the etching Amy and I had stopped with earlier in the day. It depicted a rolling sea full of dolphins playing in the water around the boat and osprey, who flew around hunting fish. In the back on the left side were two crafts. One sat too low in the water for me to read the name. The other had the name World Travelers painted on the side.

To my amazement, the same cabin cruiser showed in the picture of Ivy as she floated aimlessly with the ocean currents. I concluded it had to have seen the Iguana Veloz as it burned and most likely exploded. Or the boat's name meant something to Ivy, and she wanted to preserve it. Amy had pointed out the pictures could contain items not apparent. Maybe the World Travelers' cruiser was one of those items.

Why hadn't we noticed the ships before yesterday? Once I saw them, I couldn't un-see them. I studied the drawings with the named ships until they went out of view. I had to blink to bring them into focus once again.

The ship looked as though it was near the horizon yet the top third of the boat remained visible. The Tuckers' boat showed detail. As it would, being the center of the drawing.

My conclusion? Whoever occupied the World Travelers had something to do with the death of Ivy Tucker two months ago, and the rest of the family fifteen years earlier.

When I couldn't keep my eyes open any longer, I went back to bed. Axel dutifully came along and jumped onto the bed as I settled under the covers.

I wondered what Ryan would say about our new sleeping companion.

At first, I wondered how anyone, meaning me and Amy, could look at those pictures dozens of times and not the ship. It appeared in three of the drawings. Something my fifth-grade social studies teacher told our class popped into my mind.

I asked why the Native Americans didn't see the explorers before they reached the shore. His answer went like this—*In hundreds and hundreds of years, no one had ever approached the shore by ship.*

When you see nothing year after year, you don't look any more. It is why some people don't realize a building is being built until months, and maybe years after it is finished. People knew there was not a building in that spot, so they drove by it every day and never glanced in the direction of the construction. One day, someone asks if you have ever eaten at the restaurant? You look for it, and you could swear it was built the night before.

It was the same with me and Amy. We didn't expect to see anything else on the etchings and we didn't. It's true, at first, they were subtle, they now flashed like neon signs.

I slept late and jumped into the shower when I heard the men change shifts and Digger bark for Chili to come play. Within twenty minutes, I made it downstairs where a bagel with cream cheese and a latte waited for me on the outside table.

Amy joined me. "You're in a good mood. You must have slept well."

"On the contrary. I was up most of the night. I've concluded the World Travelers most likely saw the boat go down and said nothing to the authorities. Whoever captained that boat and the passengers killed the Tuckers, I am sure of it. I bet they picked up Michael Mannes and helped him escape."

"Or murdered him too," Amy said in a low voice. "Remember the saying, *Honor Among Thieves?* In this case honor among murderers. We need to find out where the boat was housed when it wasn't on the water. I believe we will have our killers."

I stood and looked out over the lawn. "Ever

wonder why the FBI, Mexican Police, Coast Guard, and local police never figured this out? And, if Christine Hamilton did this for revenge for her son and husband, then who is the short, dark, Hispanic looking man who poisoned you, kidnapped Ray, poisoned Ryan's men, and terrorized him and me while we were in Mexico?"

Amy snapped her fingers. "Come on guys and girls. Let's go in and get some work done. I'm ready to find the bad guys."

It isn't exactly what we did. I fed the dogs and we got another cup of coffee before we headed for the office.

Ryan called. "Hi there, I miss you. When will you be home?"

"My plane arrives at three, but I need to go straight to the office. I should be home by six. Want me to pick up takeout?"

"I spoke with Nathan earlier and he said you have found an entire new avenue to explore in the Tucker case. Besides, I've been eating some pretty good food. The CEO had me to his house twice for dinner. How about Chinese?"

"Okay. See you at sixish. I'm hungry for General Chicken, egg rolls, and crab Rangoon."

"I love you,"

"Love you, too."

"While you were lovey-dovey with Ryan, I found something. The Coast Guard doesn't know where specific boats are stored, but the nearest port is listed when the boat is registered. For instance, if we had a boat at the Lake of the Ozarks, the name of the boat and Lake of the Ozarks would be on it."

"I hope it isn't somewhere like the Lake with its five hundred or more docks."

Amy said, "Is your nose growing over there? I bet there is no more than three hundred."

We worked in silence for ten minutes or so when I jumped up and screamed, *"I found the boat."* It's out of San Diego."

"How many docks to you think there are in San Diego?" Amy asked.

"We only want the ones right on the water and big enough to accommodate a cruiser sixty-five to a hundred feet long."

"I found three with the amenities. Amy, I'll give you a choice, do you want to look up the numbers and call or fix lunch and take the dogs out?"

"I'll call the marinas."

I called lunch is ready and Amy answered, "Come here, this is too good to keep to myself."

I went back to the office. "What is it?"

"World Travelers is docked at Seaside Marina. The owners are Janice and Dwayne Johnston."

"It's a small world," I said. "Wonder what they saw?"

Amy typed something on her keyboard, and I waited. "Here is the phone number to the marina. Let's call them and ask."

"Do we know the exact date?"

"We can use the date the boat sank."

She handed me a slip of paper with the phone number. "Here, you call. I hate when you stand behind me and whisper things I should say. You make the call and ask anything you want."

Amy reached down to pet Sally, and Digger

jumped at her leg, wanting equal attention.

I turned away so I could concentrate. After I finished the call, I turned back toward Amy who now had her foot on Sally, rubbing her and both little dogs in her lap.

Axel slept quietly on the other side of my desk.

"They said they had a ledger and logged the comings and goings of the vessels. He didn't mind helping, but they switched to electronic records a few years back. He would have to go to the storage in the next building and find the book for 2005. He said it was lunch time and there were people everywhere wanting gas, asking directions, and getting lost. He said he could get the information to me by five. Nice guy."

She stood and put the dogs on the floor. I'm hungry now. Let's go."

Randy drove to Steak 'n Shake and picked up burgers, fries, and milk shakes. The next hour we basked in fast food heaven.

At five on the dot, my cell phone rang, Ryan came in from the back of the house, and Nathan walked through the front door. Digger and Chili greeted them, Axel and Sally didn't so much as twitch an ear.

Ryan opened his arms. "Don't I get so much as a hug?"

I stood and met him halfway. "I'm truly glad you are home, I've missed you."

Nathan and Amy said their hellos. "Can you be done for the night?" Ryan asked.

"You bet," Amy and I said in unison.

CHAPTER 26

Amy and Nathan did not stay to visit. Ryan and I had Chinese. We drank beer from a micro-brewery he had visited on his trip.

I snarled my lip at the label of the wheat beer. It had little yellow cartoon men fashioned out of blueberries and hats made of pineapple rings. The beer was tasty.

We retired to the living room. Axel positioned herself as close to Ryan as she could. Chili, who started out on my lap, wedged her way between us and went to sleep.

Ryan had given a presentation of his new combination alarm and drone anti-theft system to a group of business owners. They included two auto dealerships, three real estate companies, nine retail stores, and eleven warehouses. Of the twenty-five, five signed on the spot. Eight more he felt certain would use his services, and the rest were iffy except for one cantankerous old man who hated everything.

I had always prided myself on my listening skills, but the more in detail he described his adventures the more my mind wandered to my news. I put myself in his shoes and tried to get interested. It was all I could do not to sigh when he finished and asked, "What happened in the Tucker case while I was gone?"

I rattled off all of the events, the boat, the fact that the neighbor had died years before, we had tracked down the women who met us at the house, the diving company, the boat dock, and all the other facts I could remember. It was well after midnight.

We took the dogs out and walked around the yard admiring the shrubs and flowers. The night had turned cool following a thunderstorm earlier in the evening.

We took a hot shower until the water ran cold. My goal was to show Ryan how much I missed him. One minute he petted Chili, the next moment his breathing rhythm changed. He was asleep on his back still holding the dog.

I realized how tired he was when Axel jumped up and took his place at the foot of the bed and Ryan didn't stir. I moved close to him, took Chili off his chest, and replaced her with my arm.

Amy called at eight-thirty the next morning to say she had to go to the grocery store and dry cleaners before she came to work. Ryan still slept soundly so I trotted into the kitchen and made bacon, toast, and scrambled eggs.

He sat on the side of the bed when I went in,

looked up from his phone and grinned at me. "I was checking my messages. Two more companies signed." He lowered his eyes to the tray. "Is that for me? It smells wonderful."

I sat the tray next to him on the bed. "Actually, it was for my boyfriend, but my husband came home, and I had to ask him to leave."

He moved the tray to the bedside table and patted the space next to him for me to sit. "He's a very lucky fellow. Maybe I should remind you of how much I love you."

He pushed me back on the bed.

It seemed like no time before Amy rang the front doorbell.

I wasn't dressed. Ryan slipped into a pair of jeans with one knee out and his favorite tee shirt, a faded maroon Harvester with a tear on the sleeve. I threw the shirt away once, but he went to the bin and dug it out. After a two-minute shower, I slipped on shorts, a Cardinal tee, and put my unruly hair in a ponytail with my hands and held it in place with a yellow grosgrain ribbon.

Amy sat at the kitchen counter with a bagel smothered with strawberry cream cheese and a Chai Latte. "Hi, I see Ryan took good care of you."

I blushed.

He took my hand as I walked by and gave me a quick smile and a kiss on my palm. "Let me get a little breakfast and we'll get started. I'm excited to put an end to this drama."

We took our food to the Tomb. Chili stayed on Ryan's lap. Digger hung out with Chili and the big dogs went with me and Amy. As we settled, I told her, "Axel lays outside the shower door. Not the bathroom door, the shower door. If I ask him to leave, he moves about a foot away from me but no more."

"They are strange creatures, but I love them. Sally walked beside me as I bought groceries yesterday. I got some strange looks, but no one said anything."

She put her food on the table beside her desk and said, "The only information I could get from the men at the Seaside Marina yesterday was that the boat was out most of the summer. We can't get any more specific details because we aren't official government law enforcement."

"I'll call Roger. He can call the dock and get the information we need."

"They told me it must be faxed to them on a requisition form and have the signature of the person seeking the information."

"Okay, I'll see how friendly Captain Simon is this morning."

She put both hands on her belly the way I've seen many pregnant women do. "He always says, *don't hesitate to call if you need anything*, so don't hesitate."

To catch Roger up on the facts took a few minutes. He said to fax him exactly what we wanted to know and all the information as to who to send the paper to, With Amy's help, I did.

We researched what we could generally and learned each person on a boat of any kind going into Mexican waters had to have a current Visitor's Pass. I faxed Roger the information we needed to see who was issued Mexican Guest Passes in the summer of 2004.

We played the waiting game until we received the information back from Roger's office. "Let's call the Diving School and ask for Christine Hampton and see what happens."

"Amy, that's a great idea. Do you want to call or should I?"

"You do it." I called the number listed under Diving Schools in the San Diego phone directory. There were two full pages of listed schools. We chose this one because of its closeness to the marina.

Someone answered on the third ring. "Hi, are either of the Johnston's available?"

I had the phone on speaker. "No, they are rarely here anymore. They take new divers on their first outing."

"I see. Is there some way to reach them?"

"Who is this?"

"Actually, I am looking for Mrs. Johnston's sister Christine. She has a refund coming from an insurance company and I am trying to find an address to send it to her."

"Well, ma'am, I know you have the wrong people. Mrs. Johnston is an only child." She hung up.

Before we had time to discuss the new odd development, Roger called. I turned on my cell phone speaker once again. "Kate, Roger here. I couldn't get the information you requested. Both logs you want are sealed."

"Sealed by who?" I asked.

"The Federal Court of the Southwestern District of Chicago. They were sealed on July 31, 2004. I'm sorry. It's a wonder you have as much information as you do.

"I looked into Ivy Tucker's records. They are sealed also, since a month after her death. Same deal only this order went through the Federal Court, District One, St. Louis, Missouri."

I looked toward Amy before I asked. "Why would they seal them?"

"I'm not sure. Most sealed records are those of minors. Maybe it's because they are multi-country crimes. I doubt any judge will allow you a court order to release them when they won't let the St. Louis Police Department have them. You'll have to find another way to check on the ship and its excursions. There is nothing more I can do."

"Thanks, Roger, I appreciate your effort."

Amy suggested we take a break and walk around. The doctor told her not to sit over thirty-minutes at one time.

I made a salad. Amy wanted something sweet. There were no men guarding us or the house since Ryan came home. We had drone surveillance, right out of the movies. I scoured the pantry and found a box of Oreos. Amy took the entire package. "Let's try the California Department of Transportation and see if we can see a copy of their driver's license. They contain lots of information."

We took the dogs out, sat on the patio and enjoyed the first cool day we'd had in weeks. Amy munched on her cookies, I stayed lost in thought until her voice broke through. "I might be wrong about the D.O.T. I truly believe we have gotten ourselves into something over our heads. Maybe we should drop the investigation. It's clearly more than a boat accident."

I took a cookie. "No one has tried to hurt us or put bugs in our houses and cars for days".

She stared at me a long moment, her brown eyes so clear in the sunlight, they sparkled like stars. "Okay, but I need your word. If one more dangerous event happens, we quit."

"You have my word. In truth, I believe the listening devices stopped because of the dogs and our cars are clean because of Ryan's drones flying over both houses."

The afternoon turned into hours of tedious work with no results. Seems the state of California has 124354 families with the surname, Johnston. San Diego has 12865. That included 11098 with the name J or Janice and 6924 with the name D. or Dwayne.

The diving school had a listing on the internet, but it contained little information. There were at least twenty-five pictures of folks in various stages of diving. Captions under them boasted of many **adventures** and great finds under water. No pictures of the boat or the Johnston's were included.

Late in the afternoon, Amy called Divine Diving and asked for an appointment to set up lessons. They had no more room for new students until after the first of the year. It was August.

We had the address from the internet, although I began to doubt if the place existed. I put the address into the search line on Google Earth. Next I asked for a street view. "I found it," I told Amy as she sat with her feet on Sally. "14367 Bob Ridge Road. Want to see it.?"

She pulled a chair next to me and looked at the computer screen. An old two-story brick building showed on the screen. Half of the second floor had decayed and fallen to the ground after years of neglect.

On the front window it looked like it might have, at one time, had the words Divine Diving stenciled on it.

For the heck of it, I called the phone number on the internet, not the same number we called before. We listened to the message; *this number is no longer in service.*

Amy looked up the website once again. A page flashed on the screen. It pictured a hammer, saw, and screwdriver with a cartoon man standing next to them with a sign. It read, *Sorry for the inconvenience. We are down for maintenance.* And gave the defunct phone number we knew was out of service.

I had the foreboding feeling someone knew our every move without the bugs and trackers. I kept my concern to myself.

"Let's call it a day. It's after five. Where's Nathan?"

"He wanted to cook supper."

"What's he making?"

"I haven't a clue, but it will be ready by the time I get there. I'd better go. See you tomorrow."

I went to the wine cooler in the mud room and picked out a Moscato d'Asti, poured a glass, put the bottle on the counter, and the dogs and I went outside.

Axel had a funny way about him. He loved Chili yet he would sit beside me for hours if I didn't release him to play. Chili raced after him as they played tag around the yard. They came panting to the patio, got a drink of water and settled down. Chili laid on my lap and Axel near my legs.

How could we have gone through all we had? Ivy's body on the front porch, the trip to Mexico, the man at the hotel in Chicago, the bomber, and the assault on Ryan and the one on his men, the poisoning of Amy, and have all of it lead to nothing?

I didn't know Ryan came home until Chili jumped off my lap and Alex raised his head and wagged his tail. "Hi," I said as I stood to hug him. "Want a glass of wine?"

He raised his hand to show me the glass he must have filled on the way out. "It's a good thing I'm not an intruder. You were so focused on your thoughts you didn't know I was home."

"Believe me, darling, had you been here to do me harm, Axel would have you cornered."

He called the dogs to him and gave them some attention. "Want to tell me what has you in a blue funk?"

"No, maybe later. Want to raid the kitchen and cook dinner together? We haven't spent any time together lately."

"Sure, I'm starving."

Ryan sautéed chorizo and sour cream in a large skillet until the meat no longer showed pink, stemmed Portobello mushrooms and arranged them in the bottom of a baking dish.

He poured the sauce, which was now the consistency of stroganoff, over the mushrooms and we put it in the oven. Twenty minutes later we had a delicious dinner.

Ryan was relaxed and attentive. I didn't bring up the Tucker case. Tomorrow would come soon enough.

Together we washed dishes, wiped down the counters, opened another bottle of wine and went upstairs.

After a hot shower, we propped ourselves up on pillows and watched Vertigo for the tenth time. I fell asleep in his arms. Axel took his place at the end of the bed, Chili between us, and my head on Ryan's chest.

CHAPTER 27

We awoke to someone banging on the front door. Axel was down the stairs before Ryan and I had our feet on the floor. I ran to the bathroom to retrieve my robe. Ryan slipped on a shirt. The loud barking didn't seem to deter whoever wanted in.

Ryan looked out the security window. "It's two men in suits, with guns." He pressed the button on the intercom. "May I help you?

"FBI. Open the door."

"Please hold your identifications up to the window so we can see them."

We both scrutinized their credentials and agreed they were legit. "What is it you want?"

In a voice harsher than the first one, he demanded, "Call off the dog and open the door."

I called Axel off guard and put my hand down, as I did when I wanted him to accept a stranger into the house.

Ryan opened the door. Each man looked around as he stepped across the threshold. "Is there a problem?" I asked as I took the dog three steps farther away from the men.

One of the men stood at least six feet six and looked like he walked out of a GQ magazine. He had neatly combed hair and a handsome face. The other man stood no more than five feet seven and looked like he had slept in his clothes. The big man spoke. "I'm Agent Riley." He pointed to his companion. "This is Agent Marshall. We are from the St. Louis Field Office. We have a warrant to bring you in and hold you until someone from the Chicago office arrives. Please get dressed and come with us."

I looked at Ryan and then to the agents. "We need to make arrangements for the dogs. I can't just leave them here. I'll call my business partner. She will come right over."

"Would that be Amy Perkins?"

I felt my face go red; my stomach jumped. Ryan stepped close to me and rested his hand on my shoulder. "Has something happened to Amy?"

"No. At this minute FBI agents are at her home detaining her and her boyfriend. They will be at the office when you arrive. You will have to leave the dogs here or find a replacement babysitter. Whatever you decide. We need to get on with it."

Ryan glared at the men, turned around to pick up Chili who had come down the stairs and wanted to go outside. He signaled to Axel and he followed.

I slipped on a red Life is Good tee shirt and

skinny leg jeans, washed my face, took an extra long time to brush my hair. I was done and back in the living room with the officers before I saw Ryan again.

No way I would ask them to sit. They could stand and remain uncomfortable. I heard Ryan on his cell phone, but I couldn't make out the conversation. He brought the dogs in and went upstairs without so much as a glance in the men's direction.

The doorbell rang before Ryan returned. One of the agents opened it. "Who are you?" the big man said in an unfriendly voice.

"I'm David Roe. I work for Mr. Meade. He asked me to come over and babysit his dogs."

They stepped aside and let David enter.

Once I was sure David knew how to take care of things and I made sure Axel wouldn't take his arm off when we left, we went with the agents.

They stuffed us into the back of a plain Jane SUV with windows tinted so dark no one could see in. We held hands on the way to the field office. Neither of us said anything, but my mind couldn't get past two words; Ivy Tucker.

The drive downtown took an exorbitant amount of time in the St. Louis morning rush hour traffic. They drove around the six story Federal Building to an underground garage that couldn't be seen from the street.

We were escorted to the fourth floor and into a conference room with eight overstuffed chairs with rollers, a mahogany table and a serving cart in the corner with coffee and pastries. As if anyone could eat.

We looked up as Amy and Nathan were led into the room. Amy walked over to my left side and sat down. Nathan sat across the table next to Ryan.

I started to ask if they had any idea why we were here, but Nathan put a finger to his lips in a be quiet gesture. He took his fingers and walked them across the table like a bug.

We sat and waited, presumably for an FBI agent from Chicago. No one wanted anything to eat, but one by one we went to the cart and came back with a cup of coffee.

I nearly finished mine when two men entered the room and closed the door behind them.

One man, older with salt and pepper hair and a pinstriped blue suit, pale blue shirt, and a two-toned tie in dark blues; carried a heavy folder.

The other man I guessed to be about my age wore dark brown slacks, a crisp white shirt, maroon sport jacket and no tie. He carried a folder, which he laid on the table.

Each of them had an official identification card hung around their necks with GUEST in big bold black letters.

The men took seats with an empty chair between them. I'm not sure why, but I knew they sat where they did to look less intimidating like teachers at the head of the classroom.

The man with the open collar said, "I'm David Lee, Agent in Charge, of the Chicago Field Office of the FBI." He pointed to the man in the pinstriped suit. "This is Agent Mark Keeling, Special Agent in charge of multinational crimes. Mark is also with the Chicago office. You're probably wondering why we brought you down here today. We are going to explain everything."

"Don't you want to know who we are?" Amy asked.

Agent Keeling opened the manila folder in front of him and let photos fall onto the table. "I have so many surveillance photos I see your faces in my dreams." He picked up a picture of me. "Kate Nash, aka Katharine Meade, private investigator who solves crimes and mysteries but cannot keep from making headlines everywhere she goes."

Next he had a shot of Ryan leaning against a car in Mexico. "Ryan Meade, one of the richest men in St. Louis and in the top hundred in the US. Mr. Meade gets involved in his wife's escapades because he cannot bear to say no to her."

My rage built, but I remained quiet. Ryan made a fist. Amy and Nathan stirred in their chairs.

Next, a photo of Amy and Nathan together as they watched a movie in our living room. Amy Perkins, Kate's business partner and best friend, an ex-patrolman from Chicago who came to St Louis to escape a sad situation. She was raped by a suspect when he overpowered her in a dark warehouse."

Nathan's face turned crimson and the shock he couldn't hide made it clear Amy didn't tell him.

"Nathan Morris, Ryan Meade's best friend and second in command at Meade International although lately he has been assigned to the Ivy Tucker case.

"Now that we have introductions out of the way,

let's talk about the Tucker family tragedy from 2004."

"Where did you get those pictures?" I asked, as I tried to keep my voice steady and my growing anger contained.

"We'll ask the questions," Agent Lee said. "Why did you decide to investigate the murder of Ivy Tucker? Mrs. Meade, Kate Nash, you can answer the first questions."

I nodded. "When Ryan and I found the girl on our front porch, she had one of my business cards in her pocket." I glanced toward Amy who silently acknowledged my statement.

"Our first stroke of bad luck," he said. "Had she died somewhere else, she would have been quietly buried as Jane Doe and none of this would have happened."

I put my hand on Ryan's knee. He placed his hand on top of mine.

"Well, Kate. Can I call you Kate?"

I shook my head yes.

"I read your dossier."

There wasn't any way to hide my surprise. I didn't think ordinary folks had dossiers.

"You are quite a successful sleuth. You and Amy, and the two gentlemen here, found a serial killer, took down the most notorious crime family in New Jersey, and now have managed to screw up years of preparation and work for the FBI.

"Even though your friend was nearly killed by a deadly snake venom." He looked from one of us to another.

"Your husband's men assaulted and one

kidnapped, didn't deter you. Maybe we should recruit you to work for us. There aren't many agents as tenacious as the four of you."

Agent Keeling opened the manila envelope that had been inside the folder he brought with him. He handed a packet of papers to each of us. He took out a cell phone, called someone and said, *you can come in now.*

Two young executive types walked in. One a beautiful blond girl who should have been on a fashion runway instead of in an unfeminine blue suit, a man-tailored white shirt, and an obvious gun bulge under her jacket on the right side denoting her to be left-handed.

The other was a twenty something man, not particularly good looking, yet his eyes were the bluest I'd ever seen. I wondered if he had on colored contact lenses.

Keeling spoke again. "This is Agent Ames and Agent Duran. They are here to witness the signing of the affidavits you have in front of you. Read every page carefully, initial at the bottom and then pass each page to one of the agents. Ames, you take the couple on the left, Duran, the right. They pulled chairs to an appropriate spot, handed us each a pen, and sat with their hands on the table. They resembled mechanical dolls more than people.

"What are these?" Ryan asked.

"They are self-explanatory. You are about to hear facts not known to the public and should never be seen by anyone outside the agents on the case. This is an iron clad form promising us you will not repeat a word you hear today."

Nathan spoke for the first time. "Isn't our word good enough for you?"

"Sorry sir, not in this case."

The next ten minutes were quiet while we read and signed the papers. During the time we did the paperwork, a woman in a maroon dress, low heels, and salt and pepper hair came in with sandwiches, cold drinks, and chips.

They seemed friendlier, but there was nothing friendly about the papers I had in front of me. If any fact left the room we were in, we would be arrested and could spend up to seven years in a Federal prison and forfeit all our assets in the United States. One page said we could not discuss what we heard with one another.

None of us balked at signing. I knew we would not get out of the room without it.

When the papers were signed and witnessed, the two younger agents left. Agent Lee said, "Now that the tedious part is done let's take a break. I know we brought you here without breakfast or your morning coffee. Feel free to walk around, help yourself to the food. We'll take a thirty- minute break. The restrooms are down the hall, men on the right, ladies on the left."

We all remained in our seats for a long quiet moment. Chances were there were listening devices in the room. One word about Ivy Tucker or her family could land us in jail. Ryan said, "I'm going to use the bathroom and take them up on their food and drink. This could be a long day."

When the agents re-entered the room, we had all eaten a sandwich and had our choice of drinks in front of us.

"If you are ready to begin," Lee said, "had Ivy not died in such a public way, we would not be here today. Everyone, including the Mexican authorities, FBI, and US Marshalls thought Ivy drowned all those years ago. Then Samuel Carrere appeared after an absence of ten years.

"He killed the Tuckers, burned the boat, and left Ivy for dead?" Amy asked.

"No. The point is, no one killed the Tucker family. Samuel, known locally as Michael Mannes, was a Federal Ministerial Police Officer, the Mexican equivalent of the FBI.

"He had an alias in the area of Smith River and the Baja. The Tucker family was a joint effort of both countries to save the doctors Tucker. An entire year of work went into the plan to move the Tuckers to safety.

"It all went to hell when Eric Tucker insisted he take a large amount of cash with them on the trip. I know what your question now is– *what trip*?

"Sharon Tucker is the only daughter of Jose Hernandez, the notorious drug king.

"It was his idea to branch out and go into the theft and trading of organs to wealthy people all over the world. We all know that without your health you are nothing. He insisted his daughter and her husband do the surgeries and his organization would distribute the organs, not to the neediest, or the sickest, but to the ones with the most money.

"They refused. They were a perfectly normal family until the day he kidnapped Ivy and Dallas until they agreed to cooperate. They contacted us.

We arranged for them to have the heart of a grown pig that had been tagged for the meat packing plant.

"I don't think Jose wanted to kill his grandchildren, and he returned them promptly. What we did was a good and bad idea. Every other week they wanted a heart, kidney, or lung. The Tuckers just couldn't do it.

"We arranged for a witness protection program. Until it was finalized, they used pig parts. Pigs are called horizontal humans because of the size and functionality of their organs. We weren't hurting any animals, they were destined for slaughter, and it kept the circle going until we could make all the arrangements."

I put my hand up for him to stop. Amy was green and looked as if she would throw up any minute, Ryan had turned away several times, and I had never seen the look Nathan had on his face. "I know you deal with this sort of thing regularly, but the details are a little much for us all at once. We need a break before you tell us what happened to the family on the boat and how Ivy ended up with a retired nun in Mexico."

Agents Lee and Keeling whispered a few words to one another and declared a fifteen-minute break.

During our break a US Marshall joined the two agents. Once we resumed, he was introduced. He fit my picture of a movie star Marshall. I rolled it over in my head. Aaron Daley. Had it not been for the logo on his shirt and the badge holder hanging from his belt, I would have thought him a cop. Aaron had a presence. His hair, thick and blond, hung to the top of his eyebrows yet didn't look messy. His biceps bulged under a long sleeve khaki shirt, and his leg muscles strained the uniform pants. His smile seemed genuine when he came to our end of the table and shook each of our hands.

Agent Lee looked at him and said, "I'm going to turn this over to you."

The Marshall stood. "I'm not sure if you are aware, but the US Marshal Service oversees the Witness Protective Program in the States. Each family or group is assigned a handler. I am the handler for the Tucker family."

When he heard the murmurs and disbelief from us, he put up his hands. "I know it sounds completely impossible, but I will explain it to you. It is virtually never revealed who is in the program and where they are.

"We have extraordinary circumstances here. You have all signed an affidavit that nothing said in this room is ever repeated. Due to the delicate situation our participants are in, we ask you don't discuss it with one another either. I'm sure you all know by now; we can listen to anybody at any time with our equipment. It doesn't matter what you have, ours will trump yours every time"

Amy broke in. "What about the man who almost killed me with snake venom, attacked Ryan's men and stole his company car and drove it into the river? Are you trying to tell us U.S. law enforcement did that to us?"

"I haven't told you anything so far. Could you just sit still and let me talk?"

Ryan put both hands on the table, I could feel his body tense next to mine, but he said nothing.

"On June eighteenth, two thousand and four, the Tuckers were to leave on a supposed trip to the Mexican mainland by schooner. The captain was one of ours. Well, not ours. He was a member of the US Coast Guard. He had done undercover work for us before. We trusted him to do a simple job.

"He was to pair up with Marshal Jane Randall, sail the family to the whale watching site at Ignacio and three days later, take the boat further down the coast, set it on fire and let it sink.

"The three days they were in the camp, the entire family was to be picked up and moved to an undisclosed location."

I couldn't help it, I had to ask. "What about the drawings and Ivy lost on the raft. Is that a lie also?"

"No, only part of it. The Doctors Tucker insisted they have cash. It's a no-no because assets are easy to track. There was no talking Eric out of it. We hid seventy-five thousand dollars in small unmarked bills on the boat. The Federal Agent from Mexico, Samuel Carrere knew the money was with them and where we hid it.

"Once the family left the whales and began to sail, Carrere took the money and was prepared to leave. First, he sat the boat on fire."

Ryan shook his head. "What about all the blood Ivy thought she saw?"

I wondered as I looked from Ryan to Nathan to Amy if they had the same feeling I had. We were being fed a fairy tale. Why, I didn't know. All we could do was listen to the story and see how it ended.

Marshall Daley's phone rang. He went out into

the hall to answer it. When he came back all the color had drained from his face. "I must go. We will finish this tomorrow. Remember, no talking to each other or anyone else."

Amy said, "No one would believe it anyway."

He shot a hostile look over his shoulder and left.

Agent Lee took us home and said he would call in the morning to tell us what time they would come for us. Ryan said, "We'll drive ourselves, but thanks for the offer."

He took Amy and Nathan home first and then us. No one said goodbye or see you tomorrow. No one said anything.

We didn't talk about the case. Not because we were threatened, but because it was so ridiculous.

I was more exhausted than I would have been if I'd run a marathon.

We took showers, played with the dogs and went to bed. We didn't say three words to one another.

No one from the team who briefed us the day before called, emailed, or came by.

In the afternoon, someone knocked on the front door. Ryan looked out the security window of the right side of the door and I looked out the left. It answered the question as to why Axel sat relaxed at her side and Chili wiggled like a fishing worm. Ryan opened the door.

Amy sat Digger on the floor. He ran as fast as he could to Chili and they began to wrestle. Axel wagged his tail as Sally went to sit beside him.

"Hi guys," I said in my most cheerful voice. "Are you as nervous as we are, waiting for the other shoe to fall?"

Amy gave me a hug and pushed me back to look in my eyes. "I don't think there is another shoe. I believe they ran out of script for the fairy tale."

"They are most likely sitting in a room trying to find a logical way to describe all the mishaps we had. They certainly didn't fit into the story they were weaving," Nathan added.

Ryan walked toward the kitchen. "Anyone hungry or thirsty?"

We all were. Nathan made grilled cheese sandwiches. I made a salad and Ryan cut a watermelon in to triangle shaped pieces.

Just as we sat down to enjoy our lunch, someone rang the doorbell three times in a row without waiting to see if anyone would open the door. Ryan signaled for us to stay. A few minutes later, he came back and sat down. "It was a currier."

He laid two packets in the center of the table. One addressed to Amy and Nathan and one to me and Ryan. I picked the one up with our names on it and opened the package. I read aloud. *A car will pick you up at your home at nine pm. Agent David Lee, FBI*

"I wonder if ours is the same?" Nathan opened it and took out the page written on official FBI stationary. "It reads the same only ours is signed, Agent Mark Keeling."

Ryan took a bite of his sandwich and looked at each of us. "Doesn't make you feel warm and fuzzy, does it?"

"Should we go?" Amy asked. "Think it is on the up and up, or is it something else completely?"

We finished our lunch in silence. Amy and I took

the big dogs for a walk around the block. The guys moved to the patio to drink a beer. "Are you nervous about tonight?" Amy asked.

"I don't know what to think. I'll make up my mind when I see who picks us up and what they are driving."

Amy stopped to let Sally potty. "I know I'll be armed."

CHAPTER 28

I dressed as if I had a case to handle, black slacks, a white cotton tee, and a lightweight blazer to hide the Glock I shoved into my pants at the small of my back.

Ryan wore jeans, a blue tee shirt and a Cardinal jacket to cover his weapon.

Before Amy and Nathan left, we all decided the entire note seemed off along with the secrecy around it and the time of the ride. It called for caution. My common sense told me to insist I take Axel. I knew it was out of the question.

Ryan suggested we put Chili in her crate and Axel loose in the house to guard her and her surroundings. It would be a first, I reluctantly agreed.

Promptly at nine, Agent David Lee rang the doorbell. When I saw him, I let out the breath I didn't realize I'd been holding. "Sorry for all the cloak and dagger arrangements. It will all become clear later."

Agent Lee drove to Highway 40, turned on Highway 94, then Highway D and there was no longer a question of where we were headed. Busch Wildlife Area, a nearly seven-thousand-acre wildlife refuge ran alongside us on the left. I knew the area closed at ten pm. I shouldn't have worried.

The agent turned onto a road with a locked gate across it. Lee stopped the car, got out, unlocked the gate, and returned to the car. We drove about a half mile before he turned onto a smaller road to the left. A sign read Area 23, Catfish pond, No Fires, and a likeness of Smokey the Bear.

Ryan and I were in the backseat. He turned to us. "I'm going to have to insist you give me your firearms. You are in no danger."

We complied.

He led us down a pitch-black path with trees and shrubs on both sides. We came to a bunker, equally dark. He led us inside.

I knew there were a hundred such bunkers in the park. They were part of a TNT manufacturing plant during WWII, as part of the war effort.

The air in the underground open-ended concrete shelter was cold, damp, and dark. The further we walked, the brighter it became until we were in, what I guessed, the middle of the structure. Work lights were placed into a circle. They lit the space like daylight. Amy, Nathan, Agent Keeling, and Marshall Daley had taken seats around two adults who looked vaguely familiar, yet I couldn't identify.

There were three empty chairs. The three of us sat.

Daley pointed at the couple to his left. "I'd like to introduce you to Sharon and Eric Tucker."

We had seen pictures from earlier years and drawings by Ivy.

In person they were different. They were sixteen years older and secondly, they looked scared to death.

The Tuckers said nothing. They merely nodded to us.

Marshall Aaron Daley began to talk. He patted Sharon's hand. "We are here to put an end to your investigation of Ivy Tucker's death and finish explaining to you what occurred since the Tucker's left on their vacation all of those years ago.

"We stopped the meeting the other day because we saw on your faces you didn't believe a word we said." He waved his arm to encompass the agents. "Once we talked it over, we realized, we would not have believed it ourselves.

"The doctors agreed to come here at great danger to themselves to put this matter to rest. I ask that you hold any questions until the end of this meeting. We need to make this meeting as short as possible and fly them back to safety."

Sharon began, but first she put her hand on her husband's knee. "In 2003 I was approached by a wealthy man whose son needed a kidney or he would die. He and his organization kidnapped a homeless boy and wanted me to remove his heart for a rich man's son. I could not.

"My husband and I met secretly with the FBI to

see how we could best handle the situation. Apparently, this was not the first boy who needed an organ or the first child they took to sacrifice.

"There happened to be a doctor who agreed to do these procedures. He was caught, charged with the murder of several children and is now in prison. The man came to me. When I said no, they took two of our children as bargaining chips.

"Because of the deeds they perpetrated before, we knew they would kill our children, so we decided, through the authorities, to hide the children they took for organ donors and we replaced the parts in question with pig organs. Since it works well, they didn't find out.

"Our children were released, and I kept doing organ transplants for the monsters."

Eric squeezed his wife's hand and took up the story. "The reason we are here is to explain everything that happened to you and us and to beg you to not release Ivy's drawings. First, they aren't a true depiction of what happened and all the evil people on the other side of this have not been apprehended. We have two more grown children with lives of their own, new identities and it isn't fair to open this case and take a chance of the men coming after us again."

Marshall Daley went on because both Tucker's were openly spent. "The elaborate details of the trip were only to throw off the people in question. The plan was to make them think it was a family vacation.

"The man who caused you all the trouble, killed Ivy, and put your friend in the hospital was Federal

Ministerial Police Captain Samuel Carrere. He had been undercover for years as Michael Mannes.

"We used him as the captain of the schooner so the Tuckers would have protection aboard the ship. It backfired on us. Carrere's goal all along was to steal the cash hidden in the vessel and sink it with everyone aboard.

"In the middle of the night, he went below to kill the family. Ivy didn't like being closed in and always slept on deck. Eric woke up as Mannes came down the stairs and a fight ensued. He tried to take the knife from Samuel and a fight broke out. The Tucker boys tried to help. There was blood everywhere.

"When Ivy ran down the stairs, we believe, being as young as she was, she panicked at all the blood and didn't look further into it. She believed her family dead. Mannes already had the seventy-five thousand dollars in cash in the dinghy. He set the schooner on fire as he made his escape.

"From this point, we don't know what happened to Ivy. The Marshalls and Mexican authorities rescued the rest of the family, but Ivy was never found."

Sharon said, "Until you found her on your front porch, we always thought she drowned when the ship sunk."

Tears flowed down Ivy's mother's face. Her husband put his arm around her and patted her gently. Her father spoke in a low halting voice. "Not a day went by we didn't pray she would show up. The US Marshalls had new identifications for us and the kids. We had a new life set up far away from Chicago. Of course, we gave up our medical practices for fear we would be too easy to find. It all went to hell when Ivy went missing. Thus, the Divine Diving fiasco. We used it so we could dock a cruiser in the Sea of California in hopes we could locate our girl.

"To us, she died the day Marshal Daley told us about her being found. As soon as we heard how she died, we knew it was Michael or Samuel."

Dr. Tucker paused and Aaron Daley continued. "It was Michael Mannes who caused you all the trouble. He was apprehended in Mexico and shot trying to escape the Policia before he could be formally charged. The whereabouts of the money, anything he might have known about Ivy, all of it, died with him."

I stood. Both FBI agents did the same. "Hold on boys," I said. "I need to move around, nothing more. I do want to know about the man who threw the bomb into our kitchen, how the listening devices kept getting into the house and cars."

"All FBI personnel," he answered.

Ryan asked, "You expect us to believe the FBI threw an incendiary device through the window and into the kitchen?"

"Yes, he was an analyst from the St. Louis office. Had the device exploded, it contained a cherry bomb. We had no intention of letting it go off."

Before Ryan could speak again, Nathan said. "What was the point of all of it? Why didn't you come to us like you have now and tell us the truth?"

Marshall Daley, who had been sitting next to

Dwayne Tucker stood and walked behind their chairs, He put one hand on each of their shoulders. "I don't think you have a clue what it takes to make people disappear in one location and appear in another with new lives, names, birth dates, social security cards, money, and all the rest. They must cut ties with friends, family, neighbors, everyone they knew in a past life. And you." he looked straight at me, "were tracking them down, and doing a bang-up job, I might add. The neighbor who talked to you was Chicago FBI, the neighbor who said he bought the house for a bed and breakfast, a Marshall.

"Had we not tracked your every move and listened to your conversations, we would not have been able to stop you."

"What about Ivy's drawings? And if we could find the woman who cared for her, why couldn't you?" Amy asked.

Her mother said, "Ivy was a traumatized eleven-year-old girl. Her family was gone. She saw a man with a bloody knife jump off the boat, the boat sunk. Her pictures, I think, were a rendition of what she rationalized happened on that schooner. None of us were around to tell her differently." She sobbed openly now.

"Here are the options," Marshall Daley told us. "You can turn over the drawings, forget about Ivy Tucker and your investigation, forget you have seen these people, and go on with life, or you can publish the pictures with your story about what you believe happened based on the shattered mind of a child. The Tuckers can go back to the new life they have created, back to the business of living or we can begin again. That means new identities, home, and all the rest that goes with it all over again.

"The children are grown. Max is married with a baby; Dallas is in the last year at college. Their new ID would have to be without the family. They would have to never see their grandchild again or be a part of their children's lives. It would involve too many people to move them all again. I, myself, think they have suffered enough. Let this go."

I sat down while the cop talked. The four of us said nothing. Body language and having known the people next to me for so long, I knew their silence was not defiance but sorrow that we had ever found a young woman on our porch, dead. There was one more thing I needed to know. "I realize this is a small, well tiny, detail in the scheme of things, but did Captain Roger Simon of the St. Louis Homicide squad know anything about this, the bomb not being real and the menacing people being agents?"

"No, we kept everyone we could out of this. It is why the bomb squad came dressed in their suits instead of getting dressed at the scene. People are easy to fool when they are used to routine. I'm sorry about everything we had to do. But my job was and is to protect this family and I take it very seriously."

Ryan, me, Amy, and Nathan stood and walked into the darkness where we could talk in private. It had nothing to do us not intending to protect the people whose new names we didn't know. It was more about how we could phrase it, so they didn't have to look over their shoulders wondering if we used the story of their lives as entertainment to be repeated at parties.

We walked back and I told the group, "First, I want to say, from all of us, how sorry we are this happened to your family. From what we heard in Mexico by the woman who kept Ivy all those years, she was smart and beautiful.

"Next we want to say that when we leave this bunker, we will never speak of this to anyone, and not among ourselves. Not because we signed papers agreeing to it, but because you have suffered more than any family needs too.

"You needn't begin again. Enjoy your life and forget about us. When we started this investigation, we had no idea where it would lead.

"We wish you the best in all you do. I would be more than happy to turn Ivy's original drawings to Aaron so you can see them."

The Tucker's stepped forward and we all shook hands. She whispered to me. "Please destroy all the drawings and every copy you have. It would bring back more memories of my precious Ivy and the horrible childhood she endured because of Michael Mannes. God Bless you."

She took a step forward and hugged me, as well as Ryan, Amy, and Nathan.

We stood silently looking after them as they disappeared into the darkness at the other end of the bunker.

Ryan took my hand and squeezed it. Come on Private Detective Nash. Let's go home and count our blessings."

Amy put both hands on her belly. "Here, feel this."

We took turns as we each experienced the kicking and the joy of a new life.

For days, whenever I thought of the Tuckers, beautiful Ivy, and the drawings she created out of fear, I had but one thought; but by the grace of God go I.

THE END

ABOUT THE AUTHOR

Susan lives on a farm in Southwest Missouri. She loves dogs and has rescued over a dozen. The only dog at the farm that's not a rescue is Chili, a mini dachshund that becomes a character in the popular Kate Nash Mystery Series.

She writes full time in a small studio behind the barn. Her hobbies include cooking, art of any kind, walking and spending time with her family.

The Wedding Cake Murder, the first book in her cozy mystery series The Arizona Summers Mysteries, will be out later this year. And of course, it features Nutmeg a dog who might be physic.

You can follow Susan on her author page on Facebook @susankeene1author, on Twitter @susanskeene, or on her website www.susankeeneauthor.com or by email, susankeenebooks@gmail.com